Susan wished she cou̶ͅld talked to Bridget. H stance was rigid.

He'd been taut since he stepped out of Bridget's flat and caught sight of Susan. She hadn't looked at him directly, but she caught the flash of tenderness in his face, a softening that made her heart feel like mush, before he turned his back on her and marched toward Bridget with shoulders as rigid as a building wall.

Such nice shoulders.

"I love him," Susan murmured to the baby.

He cooed in response and took two fistfuls of her hair.

"But he'll never love me. He'll get his goldfinch back and leave."

The baby giggled.

Smiling, Susan cuddled him close. "I can live without him if I can make babies like you laugh."

If she could bring hope to the little ones and their parents.

"How can I do this, Lord? I don't know You enough to talk to people like Deborah talked to me, but I must do. . . something."

Her gaze strayed to Daire. Her heart had reformed itself from the ball of mush and now bounced off the wall of her chest like a ball. It hurt to have him ignore her. Physically hurt.

Award-winning author **LAURIE ALICE EAKES** has always loved books. When she ran out of available stories to entertain and encourage her, she began creating her own tales of love and adventure. In 2006 she celebrated the publication of her first hardcover novel. Much to her astonishment and delight, it won the National Readers Choice Award. Since then, she has sold eight more historical romances. A graduate of Asbury College and Seton Hill University, she lives in Texas with her husband and sundry animals.

Books by Laurie Alice Eakes

HEARTSONG PRESENTS
HP791—Better Than Gold
HP880—The Glassblower

The Heiress

Laurie Alice Eakes

Heartsong Presents

To Louise, Marylu, Paige, and Ramona, whose input makes my writing and my life so much richer.

A note from the Author:
I love to hear from my readers! You may correspond with me by writing:

Laurie Alice Eakes
Author Relations
PO Box 721
Uhrichsville, OH 44683

ISBN 978-1-60260-768-2

THE HEIRESS

All scripture quotations are taken from the King James Version of the Bible.

All of the characters and events in this book are fictitious. Any resemblance to actual persons, living or dead, or to actual events is purely coincidental.

Our mission is to publish and distribute inspirational products offering exceptional value and biblical encouragement to the masses.

PRINTED IN THE U.S.A.

one

Daire Grassick paced back and forth on the sidewalk in front of the pawnshop. He possessed only one valuable object, and the dealer didn't want to buy it.

"I've got to get home, Lord. Please." The murmured prayer sounded strange to his ears. Weeks, perhaps months, had passed since he last spoke to the Lord. He relied on his own wit and strength—and failed.

Head bowed in shame, he plodded on one more circuit of the pavement, hoping, trying to pray further, that the pawnbroker would change his mind and step outside to hail Daire back into the shop. Doors along the street opened at regular intervals, disgorging or admitting men, women, and children. They talked and laughed and skirted Daire, as though they didn't want to touch him. He supposed he did look a bit odd, a young man in fine, if somewhat rumpled clothes, striding to and fro in front of a door that remained closed, its toys and trinkets obscured behind dusty glass. His own bauble shimmered in his hands, golden glass as delicate as mist, as detailed as a snowflake, too fragile for him to carry about unprotected.

With one last hope that the secondhand shop dealer would see the ornament and step out of his store, Daire leaned against the front window and pulled the cotton wool wrapping from a bag flung over his shoulder. The scent of lilacs rose from the batting, a hint of the perfume his mother kept in the blown glass bottle shaped like a goldfinch, until she gave it to him, as his father's mother had given it to him.

"For your future wife."

The wife he'd been so certain he could win if only he left the farm in Salem County and headed for the city.

Another shudder of shame washed through him, and he shoved a strip of fabric around the bird.

"Don't break it." Two small hands in gray kid gloves curved around the sides of the goldfinch bottle. "It's beautiful."

Daire glanced up at the soft-voiced speaker and caught his breath. The bottle wasn't the only beautiful creation on the sidewalk. Eyes, the purplish blue of the flowers growing by Grandmother's summerhouse, gazed back at him from an oval face with skin so fine it resembled rare porcelain.

"May I look at it?" Without waiting for his reply, she lifted the goldfinch bottle from his hold and held it up to the sunlight. "Oh. The detail is perfect, but you can't see through it."

"Light ruins perfume. That's why it's opaque."

"I didn't know that." She turned and tilted the bottle, drawing out the beak that formed the stopper. Her nostrils flared at the strength of lilac scent rising above the odor of pavement dust and horses. "Is it empty?"

"Momma stopped using this for a perfume bottle a few years ago." Daire shifted. People were staring at them, and he thought their interaction looked unseemly. Yet if he had any chance that this young lady wished to purchase the goldfinch, he mustn't send her away.

"Is it cracked?" Her questions and gazing at the object persisted.

"No. I wouldn't try to sell a cracked perfume bottle." His tone turned indignant, and he took a deep breath to calm himself. "Momma simply chose to use the bottle for an ornament on the mantel in the parlor until she gave it to me for—" He stopped. The young lady didn't need to know about his disastrous betrothal.

"It would surely brighten up our parlor," the young lady murmured. She smiled up at him. "Where did it come from?"

"My grandfather made it." Daire couldn't keep the pride from his voice. "It's nearly fifty years old and the only one like it. It was part of the Great Exhibition at the Crystal Palace in London in '51."

"That's truly amazing." She sounded awed. "You shouldn't sell it, or be standing about with it in the middle of all these people." She held the bauble out to him. "It might get broken."

"I was hoping it would get purchased." Daire glanced at the shop. "But the broker said it's useless. I'm afraid he's right."

"Nothing that beautiful is useless, especially not if your grandfather made it." Wistfulness added smoke to the purple blue of her eyes. "If I owned something so precious, I'd keep it safe."

"Do you want to own it?" If he didn't need the money so desperately, Daire would have given the young lady the ornament right then and there, without knowing her name, without her being his future bride. Stomach knotted like a sail line, he held the goldfinch up to the sunshine as she had. "You can have it for twenty dollars."

"Twenty—" She laughed. "No wonder the broker wouldn't buy it if that's what you expected."

The trill of her mirth made Daire chuckle. "You can't blame a man for trying."

"No, but I can blame a man for dishonesty." She took a step backward. "Good day."

"Wait." Daire shot out one hand and touched the sleeve of her dress. "Why are you saying I'm dishonest?"

She tossed her head, sending maple syrup–colored curls bobbing against her cheeks. "You ask twenty dollars for a piece of glass? However pretty it is, it's not worth that much, so you really have no intention of selling."

"But I do." Daire's cheeks heated despite the coolness of the spring day. "I—need the money to get home. This is all I have other than the clothes on my back."

"I'm sorry." She gazed up at him in silence while a score of people passed them, some staring, others scurrying along and looking straight ahead.

A breeze off the harbor caught at the girl's wide skirt, lifting the ruffled blue fabric to reveal a mended bit of lace edging. Considering they stood outside a pawnshop and no maid accompanied her, Daire figured she must be heading inside to sell something of her own concealed inside her basket.

"But my troubles aren't your concern." With more care than before, Daire began to wrap the goldfinch in its protective cloth. "Maybe another broker or shopkeeper will be interested."

Except he'd tried every place in town since receiving the telegram telling him to get home as quickly as possible.

"I'm interested." She glanced at her mended ruffle. "I've never owned anything so pretty."

Words burned on the tip of Daire's tongue, the notion of telling her she owned something more than pretty and would see it if she only glanced into a mirror. But his days of wooing compliments like that ended with his last failed attempt at love and business.

"I only need enough money to get home," he said instead.

"How much?"

He told her. He expected her to laugh at him again.

Instead, she drew a threadbare silk purse from a pocket in her voluminous skirt and extracted several coins. "My aunt told me to purchase something pretty. This will fit the request."

She held out the money. Silver and one gold piece glimmered against the dull gray of her glove. With great restraint, Daire managed not to snatch the wealth from her and run to the train station.

"If you're certain." He cradled the goldfinch bottle as though it were alive and injured.

"I'm certain." She tilted her head and peered up at him from beneath gold-tipped lashes. "Are you?"

"I—um. . ." He swallowed.

Sun warmed the glass. For a heartbeat, he pictured the ornament forming at the end of his grandfather's blowpipe, the silica still hot from the furnace. The coins glittered before his eyes. The bird clung to his hands.

"I have no choice." He thrust the ornament toward her. "Take it, please. The train leaves in half an hour."

They made the exchange with care, while several passersby gawked at them and the wind, smelling of the Hudson River and smoke from the steamboats, billowed the girl's skirts against his legs. Once the goldfinch left his fingers, he felt as though he'd just sold his soul for thirty pieces of silver.

But it was only a piece of glass. A cunningly designed piece of glass, formed at the hands of a master, and only a bauble for a lady's vanity. Its purpose of gifting a beloved lady had only been for two generations, so ending with him wasn't all that serious.

He slipped the coins into the pocket of his trousers and turned away.

"Thank you." Her tone held awe. "I'll take good care of it."

"Do that." He took several paces then swung back to face her. She stood where he'd left her, her head bowed over the goldfinch, the brim of her hat obscuring her delicate features. "Give it to someone you love."

She glanced up at him and smiled. "I will."

A whistle from the harbor reminded him he needed to hurry to buy his ticket and board a train. He nodded at the girl and ran for the station. In his pocket, the coins jangled like discordant notes on a pianoforte. His bag flopped against his side, as empty as his heart.

"It's only a bauble," he told himself again and again.

In a few hours, he would be home. Reaching his father's bedside on time was worth losing the goldfinch. If Father forgave him for his failures in business and love, for selling the goldfinch instead of giving it to the love of his life, Daire could maybe forgive himself, maybe start again.

ã•

Susan Morris resisted the urge to stop on her way home and take out the bird to gaze at it one more time. Never in her life, as the fourth daughter, had she owned anything quite so pretty, so unique, so entirely hers. The young man who had sold it to her must have suffered a serious catastrophe to part with something so old and cherished.

His face had been troubled, his emerald green eyes holding a grief she'd only seen at funerals.

No young man with his looks and manners should appear that devastated. Susan wanted to give him every coin in her purse, if a lack of money was all that troubled him. She regretted not presenting him with a higher amount for the goldfinch bottle. But a lifetime of frugality insisted she negotiate for every purchase, even one as frivolous as the glass ornament tucked into her basket along with thread for her to alter one more of her elder sisters' gowns.

Maybe she should have purchased fine fabric instead of the bird. With three older sisters, she had never owned a new gown, and perhaps Aunt Susan Morris had meant her namesake great-niece should use her inheritance to buy pretty clothes made to fit her.

That she could afford to buy fabric and frivolities hadn't sunk into Susan's mind. She knew how much her great-aunt had left her, but she couldn't bring herself to visit the banker, her trustee, and find out if she could spend more than she would normally pay out of her allowance. She remained frugal with her funds the banker had given her—until she saw the stunning ornament glimmering in the hands of an equally striking young man. She couldn't wait to tell her family of her purchase. Surely, they would be in as much awe as she was and notice her instead of everything else that distracted them.

"Momma, I bought something pretty today," she rehearsed beneath her breath. "As Aunt Susan Morris told me to in her will. . . ."

Momma would be more interested in the man from whom she'd bought it, since Susan, at twenty-two, hadn't yet found herself a husband. Not quite as bad as Deborah at twenty-four, but she, at least, had a steady beau. Susan didn't have one, and she certainly wouldn't mention her attraction to the young man. He'd been catching a train out of town. Even if he hadn't, he would never find her interesting with her toast-colored hair and funny-colored eyes, too-pale skin even for fashion, and figure so thin she only wore a corset because not doing so was indecent. A man who looked like the one she'd bought the ornament from sought out ladies like her older sisters, who had china blue eyes and golden curls, fine figures and flirtatious demeanors. Susan would be left at home, playing governess to the younger two of her three brothers and whatever nieces and nephews happened to be in the house on any given day.

Thoughts of showing off her prize quickened her footfalls. Her house came into view, where it perched on the corner, a two-story brick building in need of paint on the trim, inside a wooden fence in need of whitewashing. Now that spring had come, the lawn and garden appeared more ragged than her mended ruffle.

Susan shuddered and ducked her head in a vain hope that none of the neighbors would see her enter the gate and recognize her as a member of the Morris family. The rest of the houses on their block sported fresh paint and gleaming fences, trimmed lawns and spruce gardens. One would think the Morrises were poor. Probably people thought they were with their seven children.

Three of those children, boys ranging from nine to sixteen, tossed a ball around the yard, accompanied by shouts of glee for a good catch and jeers when one of them let it drop. Paul, the youngest, called Susan's name. The ball flew in her direction. Remembering her precious burden, she spun around instead of reaching for the ball, and it smacked her on the shoulder.

"You little scamp." Tears of pain stung her eyes. "What did you do that for?"

"You were supposed to catch it." Paul looked stricken.

The other two boys slunk around the corner of the house.

Susan glanced from their retreating forms to Paul then to the sun. "Why aren't you boys in school?"

"No one made us go." Paul retrieved the ball. "You and everyone else left, except for Gran, so we just stayed home to play."

"You wait until Daddy hears of this." Susan frowned at him. "He'll make you regret playing hooky here at home."

"Aw, Sue, he won't do nothing." Paul grinned, his bright eyes dancing. "He's too busy writing another poem."

"Is that why he didn't say good morning to me?" Susan sighed. "I won't waste time telling him then. But you'll go to school tomorrow."

"Tomorrow is Saturday." Laughing, Paul scooped up his ball and ran after his older brothers.

"If you don't get an education—" Susan stopped in midcall. No sense in drawing attention to her brothers' delinquency. From the corner of her eye, she saw two neighbor ladies in their gardens and making no pretense of working on weeding or planting. They were watching the antics of the Morrises yet again.

Wishing she owned a poke bonnet that would hide her features, Susan entered the house through a front door left half open. A few leaves from last autumn had blown in through the gap, and she used the toe of her shoe to shove them over the threshold. They had a maid. Laundry and cooking for the eight Morrises still living in the house kept Bridget too busy for mundane tasks like sweeping. Susan would get the broom later. Right now she wanted to show off her new purchase.

Gran was the only family member home. She sat in her corner of the parlor, sketch pad on her knees, an array of colored chalks in a box beside her. She didn't look up when Susan entered.

"Gran, I bought something pretty today." Susan set the basket on the floor and began to unwrap the goldfinch bottle. "This young man was selling it outside a pawnshop. I was going into the haberdashery to get thread. . . ." She sighed.

The only part of Gran that moved was her hand holding a pencil. It flew across the paper in quick, decisive strokes.

"It's the prettiest thing I've ever owned," Susan murmured. "The young man said it was part of the Great Exhibition in London."

She held the bottle to the light, marveling at the rich golden color of the glass, the detail of wings and feathers. Were it not so delicate and shiny, she could imagine it taking off from her palm. And to think it was nearly fifty years old, had survived all this time for her to see and buy, a bauble good for nothing but the pleasure of its beauty.

Unless she poured perfume into it, of course. The bottle smelled of lilac. Susan thought she would prefer something crisp and clean like lemon.

"If I put this on the windowsill in my room," Susan continued, "the morning sun will make it glow."

"Hmm." Gran tore a sheet off the pad and dropped it onto the floor.

Susan set the goldfinch into its nest of cotton wool and reached for the sketch. It showed her in caricature form, her eyes double normal size, gazing at a giant bug captured between her fingers.

"Ugh." Susan dropped the picture back onto the floor. "Why a bug?"

"It's useless and destined to be smashed." Gran kept sketching. "You'd best tuck it away before the others get home."

"But I want Momma to see it."

"No, child, you don't. She'll never approve. Now run along

and get us some lunch. Bridget is busy with the laundry."

"Yes, ma'am." Susan tucked the basket behind a chair and headed for the kitchen.

Bridget, as plump as Susan was thin and as dark as the Morrises were fair, stood over the stove, stirring a pot of soup. "It'll be ready soon, Miss Susan. I made the boys hang out the sheets as punishment for not going to school."

"You should have made them go to school." Susan snatched a handful of raisins out of a bowl on the table. "They're going to end up working on the docks if they don't get an education."

"And what's wrong with working on the docks?" Bridget cast Susan a glare. "Me entire family works on the docks, and we're all respectable. Seems to me that eldest brother of yours would prefer that to his sums."

"I'm sorry. I only meant. . ." Susan turned to the table and began slicing bread. "They're supposed to be bankers like Daddy."

"And not one of them likes sitting behind a desk." Bridget banged the spoon against the side of the pot. "But speaking of supposed to dos, missy, you're supposed to be married by now."

"Tell me where I can meet young men, and I'll do so."

She knew the answer before Bridget opened her mouth. "You can go to church."

And hear about a God who noticed her as little as her own father? Susan shook her head but didn't argue. She went to church; she simply took care of the children instead of joining the adults for the service.

"I'll get started on the mending if you don't need my help here." She started to exit the kitchen.

"You can set the table for six in the dining room. Your mother and sisters said to expect them for lunch. I'll feed the children in here."

Susan carried plates and bowls into the dining room. If

Momma and the sisters were coming together, they must have been off on one of their charitable projects and planned to do something else that afternoon. She tried to remember what drew their interest this month. India? Yes, that was it. They were sewing clothes for the orphans in India. Susan's sewing had been deemed not good enough. A glance at her badly mended ruffle reminded her they were right.

Bad at sewing and worse at being a Christian, Susan took comfort in knowing she'd done well with her purchase. She recognized beauty when she saw it.

The sound of female voices in the hall drew her out of the dining room, the table half laid, to join her mother and older sisters. As though she were a hat stand, they piled their straw bonnets into her arms and continued their conversation about packing boxes for India.

"We must line them with oilcloth," said Daisy, the eldest. "That will protect them from sea damp."

"That much oilcloth will be expensive," Momma said. "But if we—"

"I bought something special today," Susan broke in. "It was part of the Great Exhibition in London. You know, the Crystal Palace."

Her four relations glanced at her. "For the orphans?" asked Opal, her next to the eldest sister.

"No, for me, as Aunt Morris told me to." Before they could say more, Susan darted into the parlor and retrieved the basket.

Gran held up another sketch. This one showed Momma and Susan's older sisters upside down in a packing crate.

Susan laughed. "Gran, you should make cartoons for a newspaper. People would pay money to have these."

"That would take all the fun out of it." Gran chuckled. "Is lunch ready?"

"Yes. Do you need my help rising?"

The basket with the goldfinch in it slung over one arm,

Susan held out her hands to assist Gran to her feet. Arthritis crippled her knees so badly she could scarcely walk, but she refused to use a cane or bath chair, preferring that her youngest granddaughter supported her from room to room. They crept toward the dining room, where the others still chattered about packing crates and shipping costs.

"We need another bazaar to raise money to pay for the shipping costs." Momma pulled out her chair. "Daisy, you ask the blessing."

Daisy prayed over the food that hadn't come from the kitchen yet. They all sat. Clattering of crockery from the kitchen suggested that Bridget would serve soon, so Susan pulled the goldfinch bottle from the basket before Momma and the others resumed their dialogue.

"Look what I bought today." She held the ornament to the light, wishing sunshine came through these windows to show the bird to its best advantage.

Everyone stared at it in silence.

"A young man was holding it up outside the pawnshop, and I just had to have it." Susan's voice squeaked into the stillness. "Aunt Morris said to buy something pretty."

"Aunt Morris never should have entrusted you with her fortune." Opal shook her head. "We all said you'd waste it, and look what you've done."

"Sell it," Momma directed. "It'll help pay for the shipping cost to India."

"I can donate money for that—"

"Sell it," everyone chorused.

"That'll help us get materials to make things for a bazaar to raise more money," piped up Deborah.

"But I've never owned anything. . . ." Susan slumped beneath their china blue stares, joy in her purchase draining from her. "All right. I'll see if I can find someone to buy it."

Her heart a leaden weight in her chest, Susan rose, carried the goldfinch bottle to the mantel, and stuck it behind

Daisy's wedding photograph. Out of sight, out of mind—something to forget like the young man from whom she'd made the purchase.

two

Halfway up the drive to the Grassick farmhouse, Daire reined in the mount he'd hired in town and sat staring at the array of vehicles crowding the gravel lane. Broughams, landaulets, and buggies lay cheek by jowl from the trees on one side to sweeping pastureland on the other. Horses filled the pasture, a few familiar to Daire as the teams of neighbors. Beyond the vehicles, smoke poured from the kitchen chimney, and the aroma of roasting meat permeated the evening air.

The Grassicks were entertaining what appeared to be most of the county.

"No. No." He slid to the ground then stood with one arm draped over the gelding's withers for support. "No Father, no."

He didn't know if he prayed to Father God, who couldn't be much interested in the grief Daire had brought upon himself, or if he called out to his earthly parent now gone beyond hearing him.

Either way, he feared the answer was, "Yes son, yes."

According to the telegram Daire received, his father lay near death, the victim of a bad-tempered bull, who had gored him and tossed him a dozen feet. Two days later, Daire knew of only one event that accounted for so many vehicles cluttering the drive—a funeral. He was too late to obtain his father's forgiveness.

"If only I had the money. . . ." He leaned his head against the horse's neck, a shudder racing through him.

How he'd finally obtained the means to get home would make the rest of them dislike him.

If the coins he'd received from the pretty young lady wanting to buy something frivolous hadn't all gone to purchasing his way home, he would have climbed astride the hired hack again and ridden away, kept riding until he or the horse collapsed from exhaustion. He didn't know how he could face any of his family, but face them he must.

Feeling as though his boots had turned to millstones around his feet, he trudged around the house to the stable and left the gelding with a youth he didn't recognize. "Treat him well. He may have to travel again soon."

He turned away and scanned the house. A brush against his ankles drew his attention downward. Two black-and-white cats rubbed around his legs, meowing and purring their recognition. He stooped and gave them each a pat and a scratch behind the ears. "Good beasties. You never forget a free bit of fish, do you?"

He glanced toward the kitchen door, where he, too, had obtained many a treat over the years. If he slipped in that way, he might be able to avoid the bulk of the guests and find a member of his family to break the news that he had come home at last.

Too late. Too late. Too late.

The words pounding through him with each heartbeat, he left the cats to their own devices and headed for the kitchen door. Beyond the panels, women talked and laughed and called orders to one another. Mixed with the aroma of roasting meat, cinnamon, cloves, and nutmeg swirled around the door frame like a wreath. Daire's mouth watered. His stomach growled.

A cat meowed at his feet and slipped inside ahead of him.

"Get that animal out of here," a woman shrieked. "I nearly dropped the ham. Who let the—" She glanced at Daire from beneath a ruffled white cap. "No guests in the kitchen. You'll get fed when everyone else does. Go around to the front door."

Daire stared at the strange lady, a cook or housekeeper, judging by from her black gown and white apron. He hadn't expected a fatted calf to be killed to welcome him home, not under these circumstances. Neither had he expected to be shooed away.

"Take that cat out of here and go around to the front," the woman directed again. "Please."

Daire glanced around the room for a face he recognized. No one among the three maids and one scullion engaged in various stages of food preparation appeared familiar. They gave him blank stares in return.

"I'm just passing through." He shooed the cat outside then wended his way through the kitchen staff, finally reaching the door leading to the entry hall.

What sounded like a hundred people talked and laughed behind it. The talk didn't surprise him. Grassicks were sociable people. But the laughter seemed odd for such an occasion. Yet maybe not. Father had been full of joy. The only time Daire remembered seeing him sad was when he said good-bye to his eldest son.

Burdened by this last memory of his father, Daire pushed through the swinging door and stepped into the hall. Men in frock coats and bright waistcoats and women in bell-shaped skirts swept past him. Not one looked in his direction, not even his sister. She stood five feet from him chattering and gesturing to one of the apprentices from the glassworks.

Daire leaned against the wall like a fallen portrait. Even if he didn't expect the homecoming welcome of the prodigal son, he also didn't expect no one to notice him in their midst. If he slipped up the steps to his bedchamber, perhaps he could make himself presentable, wash away the travel dust, before he needed to face them, face the truth.

He couldn't find the energy to move. Every drop of blood seemed drained from his limbs.

The kitchen door flew open and smacked him on the shoulder. He jumped and knocked the platter of sliced meat from the maid's hands. Food and crockery smashed against the floorboards. The girl shrieked. Conversations ceased, and footfalls rushed along the hall.

Face hot, Daire dropped to his knees to help gather up the mess. He had everyone's attention now.

Above him, someone gasped. "Daire. Grandma, it's Daire." His sister, Maggie, dropped onto the floor beside him, heedless of meat juice staining her gown, and flung her arms around his neck. "Oh, Daire, I thought we'd never see you again when you didn't come to see Daddy. We were so worried. He was so worried." Crying, she buried her face against his shoulder, her high-piled red curls tickling his nose.

"I got here as fast as I could." He stroked Maggie's vibrant hair. "I'm sorry it took me so long." He swallowed against the tightness in his throat. "Too long."

"But not long enough to keep away from my party." The jovial tones of Jock, his youngest brother, rang through the hall. "I can't have everything my way."

Confused, Daire glanced up. "Party? But I thought—" Warmth spreading through him, he glanced at the gathering guests and family.

None wore the somber hues of mourning. Maggie wore green the color of her eyes, the color of all the Grassicks' eyes. Jock's waistcoat sported green and gold stripes, and the stunning young lady beside him glowed in a gown of crimson and gold.

"Are you saying this isn't a—a—" Daire shot to his feet, broken china and ruined meat forgotten. "Father?"

"He's in his room resting as comfortably as possible," Maggie said. "We thought we were going to lose him, but he's on the mend, so we went ahead with Jock's engagement party. But you haven't met Violet yet, have you?"

"No, but please. . ." Daire offered the pretty young lady a smile. "I'm not fit for a celebration. Traveling. . ." He glanced about for a way to extricate himself from the staring family, neighbors, and strangers. "May I see Father?"

Would Father want to see him?

He pressed his hands against his legs to stop himself from dashing up the steps to his father's room. "I came back to see him."

"Aye, and see him you will." Grandpa's voice, still holding its Scots burr after nearly fifty years in America, pushed through the crowd and grasped Daire's hand in both of his. "Now we've three grand things to celebrate."

"Four, if you count the—" Maggie gasped as Jock elbowed her in the ribs.

"Thank you, sir." Daire coughed. "I don't deserve to be celebrated."

"Aye, but you do." Grandpa slipped his still burly arm around Daire's shoulders. "The lost lamb has returned. But he looks tired, so if you'll be excusing us, I'll take him up to his father."

Murmuring and smiling, the crowd made a path clear to the steps. Daire preceded Grandpa up the treads. His leg muscles spasmed as though he were the old man of seventy-eight and not a young one of twenty-five. At the top of the steps, Daire stopped, his gaze fixed on Father's closed door. "Maybe I should change my clothes first."

"Nay, he'll want to see you now." Grandpa laid his hand on Daire's shoulder. "You ken he'll forgive you, lad. Whatever kept you from us, 'tis not too much to forgive."

"Easy to say when failure has never been a part of this family." Daire squared his shoulders and marched toward the door.

Voices murmured on the other side of the panel: Father's distinct, if somewhat weak, and Momma's gentle, loving.

Daire's hand shook on the faceted glass knob. "This is new."

"Aye, 'tis Jock's design."

"It's a handsome piece, as fine as anything I saw in the city."

"It turns well, too." Grandpa nudged Daire. "Try it."

Daire obeyed. The knob twisted with a light touch. The door swung inward to reveal Momma lighting a lamp beside the bed. The flame emphasized her still golden hair and smooth complexion. Propped on pillows against the headboard, Father didn't fare so well. His skin shown pale beneath his normally ruddy complexion, and new threads of silver streaked his dark hair. But the Grassick green eyes still shone brightly.

They widened and blurred at Daire's entrance. "My son, you've returned."

"If you'll have me." Daire managed a smile.

For response, Father held out one hand. The other lay limp and bandaged atop the coverlet.

One arm was enough for Daire. He crossed the carpet in a handful of strides and clasped Father's hand. "I got here as soon as I could."

"You should have come home sooner." Father blinked hard, and his eyes cleared. "I didn't like having to get myself gored just to get you back."

"I'm glad my telegram found you." Momma hugged Daire. "I was afraid you'd moved on, it had been so long since we heard from you. And when you didn't come right away. . ."

"I'm sorry for the delay." Daire released Father's hand and clasped his fingers behind his back. His face heated. "I had difficulty coming up with the money to get here."

There, the truth was out, admission of his failure to succeed on his own. And he'd made the confession in front of more than his parents and grandfather. Voices in the corridor outside the bedroom warned him that his brothers, grandmother, and sister had come to join the family reunion.

Daire wondered if he could simply crawl under the bed and hide. But he'd been running and hiding for six months. He needed to face the consequences of his bad decisions and work out a way to win his way back into worthiness to be a part of this godly and gifted family.

"You should have let us know," Momma said. "We could have arranged for you to get money up there."

Daire swallowed and avoided her eyes. "I didn't have the funds for a telegram."

In the ensuing silence, someone gasped. No one asked him what had happened to the money Father had given him for investments in the city. No one asked him what had happened to his relationship with the young lady, whose family had lured him north. They didn't need to. His lack of money or a fiancée told their own tale.

"Then how did you get here?" Maggie asked.

It was the question Daire didn't want to answer.

He kept his gaze on Father. "I had to sell something."

"Like what?" Maggie pressed.

"Let the lad alone." Grandma's voice entered the crowd behind Daire. "He looks tired and hungry. When did you last eat, Daire?"

"Awhile ago." His stomach, empty since he left the city, growled.

"Take him down for a good meal," Momma suggested. "We can talk more later."

"Maybe he'd prefer to change his clothes." Jock chuckled. "He looks a little dusty."

"No, I'm not fit for a party." Daire touched Father's hand again. "And you look tired, sir. If I may come back later?"

"You may return at any time, son." Father smiled. "Whatever you tell me, it doesn't matter now that you're here."

"I wish that were true." Daire compressed his lips. "But thank you."

Heart lighter despite the shame of his past behavior, he turned to leave the bedroom. For the first time, he noticed that Jordan, his quiet second brother, had also joined the family group. He caught Daire's hand and shook it without saying a word but showing support and kindness with that single gesture.

"Daire." Maggie grasped his other arm. "It's terrible you were so badly off. How did it happen? I mean, where's Lucinda and—"

"Later, Maggie," Jordan murmured.

"But—" She sighed and released her hold on Daire. "That's right. You're home, and that's what matters most. Well, bringing the goldfinch home, too, of course."

"I didn't bring it home." Daire spoke quickly to get the moment over with as quickly as possible. "I had to sell it to pay for my fare home."

Silence filled the room, a silence profound enough to make conversation and the clink of silver on glassware below stairs audible through the closed bedroom door. But the glances exchanged between family members spoke volumes—shock, dismay, even anger.

Daire backed against a bedpost as though each look were a blow. "I knew you all would be disappointed. I mean, I know this is an important piece to the family, but its value isn't that high on the market, I learned, and any one of you can make another one."

"Aye, lad, we can make another one," Grandfather confirmed. "'Tis naught more than a bauble after all, whatever the sentiment attached to it. But 'tis what's inside the bottle that matters."

"What's inside?" Daire blinked, trying to push fatigue away. Surely his confusion lay in weariness, not in the fact that what Grandfather said made no sense to him. "The bottle was empty."

"Not precisely." Jock scowled, but at Maggie, not Daire. "Our little sister put something in there the moment it was entrusted to her."

"I didn't know Daire would run off like he did and take the goldfinch with him. I thought it would be the best place for it, like in that story by Mr. Poe—hidden in plain sight."

"You entrusted a family treasure to a tale by a dissolute

poet." Jock's voice rose. "Fiction, Mag—"

"Well, Momma entrusted the goldfinch to Daire," Maggie shot back, "and look what he—" She slapped her hand across her mouth. Her eyes filled with tears.

"You can apologize to your mother and your brother later." Father's voice drifted from the bed, weak but in command. "Right now, I suggest you keep your mouth shut before it gets you into more trouble."

"Her lips have more talent for glassblowing than for speaking," Jordan said.

"If you please"—Daire spoke between stiff lips to hold back anger swelling in his chest—"will someone tell me what this is all about, or am I to be indicted by my family without knowing the charges?"

"Nay, lad, no one is indicting you." Grandfather slung a burly arm across Daire's shoulders. "You did not ken what wee Maggie had slipped into the bottle, since you do not work at the glasshouse."

Daire stiffened. That comment in itself felt like an indictment. His younger sister worked as a glassblower, though few females did, alongside his grandfather, brothers, and several uncles. He was the only one in his generation who showed no talent for the art. His father hadn't been a glassblower either. He preferred to work the land. And because Daire showed no aptitude for farming, he'd tried his hand at business—and had been swindled.

"And we didn't dare write you about the problem with the goldfinch once you'd gone with it," Momma added.

"In other words, I'm the only member of the family who doesn't know what the difficulty here is." Daire feared a hint of bitterness had crept into his tone, and he swallowed to clear it away. "May I know now?"

"You have to," Jordan said, "so you can retrieve it from the goldfinch."

"Retrieve what?" Daire persisted.

"A formula," Jordan explained.

"For the special crystal we displayed at the Great Exhibition in London seven years ago," Jock added.

"You ken how Queen Victoria was so taken with it?" Grandfather began.

"Taken with you is more like it." Despite her seventy years, Grandmomma's eyes still shimmered amber gold when she was trying not to laugh.

"Aye, well. . ." Grandfather cleared his throat. "She has a liking for the Scots and wanted that crystal for her wee castle at Balmoral."

"But she's broken a piece," Maggie burst out, as though too many words had piled up for her to hold them back. "And I got to help make the parison for the new pieces. But the formula has been such a secret, I wanted to hide it. And we had company arrive unexpectedly one day when I had forgotten to put the formula back in the safe at the glassworks, so I rolled up the paper—it is just a little slip—into a little tube and stuffed it down the neck of the goldfinch."

"And how do you think we'll get it out without breaking the—"

"Tweezers," Maggie interrupted Jock again. "I wouldn't have done it if I thought we'd have to break—"

"And not destroy—"

"Not another word out of either of you until I say so." Once more, Father's voice rose from the bed. "Father, please finish."

"We got word last week that we need to make even more pieces," Grandfather complied. "And we do not wish to depend on anyone's memory for the exact formula, as we all recall it just a wee bit differently."

"And without the formula?" Daire asked, his stomach clenching. "What will happen?"

"We'll be in breach of contract to the Queen of England," Grandfather said, "as we got that order under the condition we would always be able to make replacement pieces for Balmoral."

Daire didn't need to ask what breach of contract with Queen Victoria meant—ruin for the company. And, worse, with the way Jock and Maggie had been speaking to, and now glared at, one another, the loss of the formula because of Maggie's carelessness first and now Daire's further irresponsibility, meant strife within the family, possibly an irreparable rift.

"But you can get the formula back," Jordan said.

"I don't know." Daire felt sick at how his gullibility and pride could so easily ruin his family. "I don't know the name or address of the lady who bought it."

three

Susan stared across the mahogany desk at the bank manager. "What do you mean you can't give me more money? Isn't it mine?"

"Yes, Miss Morris, but under the terms of your aunt's will, you can only spend this money on yourself." The banker, at a different financial institution than the one at which Daddy worked, gave her an indulgent smile. "Per her instructions, I've set up accounts for you at dressmakers and hatters and cobblers. You can buy all the pretty clothes you like, and even some jewelry, but you can't spend your money on shipping crates."

"I don't like this." Susan twisted her gloves between her fingers, noticing one finger was about to split at the seam. "I don't want pretty clothes. That is—" She glanced down at her dress, another hand-me-down from Deborah, a blue that matched her sister's eyes but made hers look like sickly lilacs. "One or two would be nice, but the children in India need things more than I do."

"And 10 percent of your quarterly interest payments went to the church." The bank manager took a sheet of paper from a desk drawer. "If you want to specify that the church use the money for mission projects, we can arrange for that for the next payment."

"Which is nearly two months off." Susan sighed. "But let's see to that. The children will just have to wait."

The children would wait even longer for assistance, while she indulged herself with pretty clothes and useless baubles. Momma and her sisters would never approve. They would continue to criticize her for buying the goldfinch bottle.

She'd tried to sell it, but no one wanted it or insisted on paying no more than a few pennies for it. So she shoved it behind the wedding picture again and approached the bank manager about giving her enough of her inheritance to pay for packing crates and shipping costs.

"Why was my aunt so insistent I fritter away this money?" Susan demanded.

The banker's smile turned gentle. "She wanted you to be happy, Miss Morris."

"What do you mean? Am I expected to buy happiness?" Tears blurred her eyes. "Was she happy with all her wealth?"

"She was, but she was happy before she obtained her wealth." The manager stood. "I'll draw up that agreement and have you come back to sign it in a day or two. I'm sorry I can't do more for you now in the way of cash, other than your allowance, but do make some purchases of things you want. Tell the store clerks to send the accounts to me."

Susan nodded, rose, and allowed him to escort her through the quiet lobby of the bank. The tellers and customers—all men—gazed at her, a young female alone in a financial institution, being treated like royalty by the manager, yet wearing a shabby dress. Her cheeks heated at the attention. It wasn't the sort she wanted.

She wanted Momma's and her sisters' approval. She wanted them to ask her to join in their charity work. Even if she couldn't sew, she could do something useful like play the pianoforte while they worked. Her musical ability wasn't terrible. She could make them cups of tea and serve them Bridget's cookies. But they didn't eat while working for fear of soiling the fabric, and they said the pianoforte music interfered with conversation.

Reluctant to go home to a house empty of everyone except for Gran and Bridget, since she'd gotten the boys off to school that morning, she stopped and made one purchase— new gloves. A hat with frothy pink netting and ribbons caught her eye. The color suited her better than the endless blue from her sisters, so she bought that, too. Then she noticed the darn on her right stocking was giving her a blister on her heel, so she indulged in two pair of fine lisle hose and delicate lace garters.

Though light, the purchases felt as heavy as the burden Christian carried in *Pilgrim's Progress*. Maybe if she bought gifts for the family she wouldn't feel so guilty about spending money on herself.

A stationer's shop drew her inside to obtain paper and pastels for Gran and a new notebook for Daddy to write down his poems. Candy for the boys completed her spending. She couldn't work out what Momma or her sisters would like. They preferred doing good works, except for buying the pretty clothes their husbands or Momma insisted they wear. They claimed one could raise more money if one didn't look like it was for oneself.

All the way home, she racked her brain to work out what she could do. By the time they arrived for lunch, she knew what it was.

"I'll watch the children on your nannies' days off," she announced. "That way, Deborah can help you, too."

Four pairs of bright blue eyes stared at her.

"You want to look after all six of our children?" Daisy asked.

"I'm good with the children at church," Susan pointed out. "They scarcely ever cry."

"It would be rather nice," Opal admitted. "Tomorrow?"

Basking in her second sister's approval, Susan nodded with enthusiasm.

Enthusiasm that died as her sisters arrived with their broods. Daisy had presented her husband with three boys, and Opal had three girls. They deposited the horde in the middle of the parlor and swept off to decorate the church hall for someone's wedding. The next one, they all believed, would be Deborah's, though her beau hadn't proposed to her in three years of courtship.

"What have I done?" Susan groaned.

She gazed at the mob of children from ages one to ten and wondered what she'd been thinking. Maybe that a school day would be the nannies' days off and half of the children would be under someone else's care.

"Paul, Roger, Samuel?" she called to her brothers, wherever they were. "Come help."

Paul and Roger, the two younger boys, thundered down the steps. Paul was the same age as his eldest nephew, but Roger, at fourteen, balked at playing nursemaid.

"Sam isn't here," Roger said, referring to their eldest brother.

"Where is he?"

Susan hadn't noticed him leaving the house that morning.

"Off to the harbor to watch the ships." Roger's lavender gaze tracked to the street. "He wouldn't let me come with him, but I want to go. There's a ship in from the Far East, and I want to see what kinds of things it brought back."

"You're too young to go to the docks alone."

So was Sam. Someone should have stopped him, but evidently no one had even noticed him leaving.

Sighing, she began to bribe Roger to help corral their nieces and nephews into the back garden and form up games. If running about in the May sunshine for an hour wouldn't fatigue them enough for naps, Susan knew it would make her drop where she stood. After a quarter hour, her hair had come loose from its chignon and hung down her back like a schoolgirl's. Grass stains marred her blue muslin skirt from several little ones tackling her to the ground, and a tumble into a rosebush had left a long, red scratch on her hand. But she was laughing.

Until she noticed she wasn't alone in the yard with the children.

Poised on the balls of his feet, as though he intended to

race off at a moment's notice, a man stood between a lilac bush and a rose trellis. The former shot fragrant blossoms in haphazard profusion halfway across the walk, and the latter threatened to topple over and bury the unwary in a profusion of thorns. They shaded the man's features, but something about the lift of his strong chin and set of his broad shoulders struck a chord of familiarity in Susan.

Extricating herself from the clutches of her youngest nephew, she took a step forward. The man removed his hat, and a bubble of joy warmed her heart as much as the sun warmed her skin. He was familiar. Not even in the shadow of overgrown flowers could she mistake those brilliant green eyes and the perfect wave of the thick black hair, his high-bridged nose, and broad cheekbones.

The handsome young man with the goldfinch bottle had found her.

&

Daire Grassick stared at the scene before him. When no one had answered his knock, the cacophony of children at play had drawn him around the house to the back garden. There, amid a jumble of children, he caught sight of one female who appeared older than the rest, though her stained gown and disordered hair were more appropriate for a schoolgirl half the young woman's age. Yet the rich golden brown of the waist-length tresses and glowing countenance assured him she was indeed the young woman who had been so happy to purchase his family treasure, more of a bona fide treasure than its sentimental value. When she drew nearer, her footsteps hesitant, her hands held before her as though warding off danger, he saw her eyes. Wisteria, Grandma had told him the flowers were called when he asked her about the purplish blue blossoms. Wisteria.

Behind her, the children ceased their play and stood or sprawled in a tableau of curious faces, except for a toddler, who stared at a laden lilac bush. Only the young lady moved.

Miss Susan Morris, according to the shop girl who'd put a name to his description. She glided across the overly long grass, a torn flounce trailing behind like a train, and that shining expression of joy he'd noticed upon their previous meeting lit her delicate features even in the shade.

"Miss Morris?" Daire stepped forward to greet her.

His arm brushed the lilac bush, sending a cascade of blossoms into the air. They clung to his coat, his trousers, his hair.

"I'm Susan Morris, yes." She swept her hand over his sleeve, removing the petals and sending a jolt like a lightning streak through him.

He swallowed against a sudden dryness in his mouth. "I'm Daire Grassick."

"I'm pleased to meet you." She held out her hand. She wore no gloves as she had in town, and he noticed the long, red scratches and a hint of roughness around the short nails, as though she was not a lady of leisure. "That is, we have already met, in a way, have we not?"

"Yes." Daire shook her hand and experienced that tingle again, an awareness of being near a pretty girl and something more he couldn't put a name to. "I've had a time of it finding you."

"I expect you did." She gestured to the children, who resumed their game with a ball and much yelling. "I don't look like the rest of my family, except for my father. But that's neither here nor there. You found me." Her voice turned breathy, like someone who'd been running, and her eyes glowed. "How may I— *Oomph.*"

The ball sailed past the toddler and struck Miss Morris between the shoulder blades. She staggered forward, caught her toe in the hem of her bedraggled skirt, and fell against him.

Daire caught her in his arms and held her a little too tightly to ensure she regained her balance. She pushed her hands to his chest so hard he swayed back against the rose trellis. Thorns caught in his coat and held him captive. The children shrieked with laughter. Miss Morris groaned and flung her hands over her face. Behind her, one of the older boys raced up, grabbed the ball, and streaked back to his companions, still laughing, apparently unconcerned whether the young lady had been injured or was in danger from this stranger who embraced her so improperly, whatever his good intentions.

"Are you hurt?" Daire asked for lack of anything better to say.

She shook her head, sending maple-syrup hair cascading around her shoulders.

"Then perhaps you could assist me."

"You?" She peeked at him from over her fingertips. "Oh no." Her eyes widened and she dropped her hands. Her cheeks had turned the color of a sunset. "I am so sorry. Here, don't move."

"I won't," Daire drawled.

"No no, you don't want to ruin your beautiful coat." She scurried around to his side and rested one hand on his shoulder. "This will take awhile."

"Perhaps one of the boys should do this."

He didn't like her standing so close to him. He'd made enough mistakes in the past six months. He didn't need to add to his bad behavior with attraction to a female about whom he knew almost nothing. He did know, however, that the shabby appearance of the girl and her house didn't make sense when he considered how much she'd paid for the goldfinch bottle. Surely this family couldn't be as poor as they looked.

"They're young," Daire remarked on the children, "but—"

"Don't move." She increased the pressure on his shoulder. "This trellis is about to fall."

"If one of those boys could hold it up, it might be safer."

"No, it wouldn't." She glanced toward the throng of youngsters.

They showed no interest in him or Miss Morris. All but the littlest one seemed engaged in a game of tag. The baby had curled up in a patch of sunlight near the lilac bush and fallen asleep like a kitten.

"They're all too young to be responsible." She made a hissing sound through her lips, and the wooden latticework frame for the climbing roses rattled. "I could get my eldest brother—he's sixteen. But Roger, one of my other brothers, said Sam's gone down to the docks. I don't know that for sure. We haven't seen him today."

"You haven't seen one of your brothers?" He couldn't keep the astonishment from his voice. "How is that possible?"

She laughed. "The rest of them are here. But it's all right. I can manage—ah, it's not as bad as I feared. Just one—ouch."

"Miss Morris?" He tried to twist his head around so he could see what she was doing.

"No, don't move. It's just a scratch, I think. There." She released her hold on him and glanced at him through a curtain of hair. "You're free now."

He wasn't free with those pretty wisteria blue eyes gazing at him through a waterfall of burnished gold. He felt bound to her by an invisible thread.

He stiffened and cleared his throat. He must get his mission accomplished and return home before temptation took over his life again. Six months was more than enough to abandon his family and his Christian faith. It brought nothing but disaster, and this girl was the culmination of that time. He must put it behind him, and that meant putting her behind him, however pretty she was. However sweet and soft her voice. However fragrant her hair and—

He stepped away from her. "I apologize for barging in on your day, Miss Morris. With your permission, I'll conclude my business quickly and be on my way."

"Business?" A shadow darkened her eyes, and she turned her head so she looked past his shoulder to the boisterous crowd of children. "Of course. I assume this has something to do with the goldfinch bottle? I mean, it's the only business transaction we have shared."

"Yes." Daire tried not to cringe at the sudden coolness of her tone. "I wish to buy it back."

With money his father had given him. More money than he'd received to go out on his own, making him worse than the prodigal; this wasn't even part of his inheritance. Of course, what that bottle held *was* part of his inheritance.

"You do?" She spun toward the house on her heel, sending the ends of her hair flying out like fringe on a shawl. "Come inside and I'll wrap it up for you."

Daire hastened to catch up with her. "You don't want to negotiate a price for it?"

"Why would I do that?" She rounded the front of the house and trotted up a set of porch steps in need of a good sweeping. "We both know how much I paid you for it. So I expect that's what you'll give me in—"

The grate of ripping fabric interrupted her.

Daire glanced down to see he'd stepped on her torn ruffle. His face flamed. If he didn't want the goldfinch bottle back so badly, he would have raced for the front gate and fled back to the train station to ride as far away from this slapdash female as he could before he committed some other faux pas beyond holding her in his arms, even if it was just to catch her from falling, making her scratch herself extricating him from rose thorns, and now ripping the bottom of her dress far enough to reveal a grass-stained underskirt.

"Perhaps I'd better wait out here," he murmured. "Since there's no one at home inside the house."

"There isn't?" She glanced back at him, her cheeks the color of June roses. "Gran surely is. But she wouldn't come to the door. Walking is too difficult for her." She glanced down. "If you remove your foot, we can go into the parlor while I get the goldfinch."

"Uh, yes, my apologies." Sure his entire body was blushing, Daire backed up.

He expected her to secure the ruffle somehow. Instead, she grasped it in both hands and yanked until it tore off the rest of the way.

"I never liked this dress anyway," she said, head down. "Blue makes my eyes a funny color."

Her eyes a funny color? If she meant not boring plain blue, then she was right. But surely she didn't believe something was wrong with the color of her eyes.

Daire shook his head. "Miss Morris. . ." He stopped. He mustn't give a female compliments. She belonged to this city, where he'd met nothing but trouble. He wouldn't encourage friendliness. He just wanted away, back to the safety of home, formula in hand to stop the bickering between Jock and Maggie and the rest of the family silently siding with Jock.

"Come inside." The bundle of fabric in her hand, she opened the front door.

The cool interior of the house displayed as much neglect as the outside. Dust gathered on picture frames. The molding needed paint. And the room most people would save for their guest parlor looked more like a nursery than a chamber for receiving visitors. Lead soldiers lay scattered about the floor like casualties of a battle, a half-full glass of milk stood spoiling on the mantel, and an old lady perched on a straight-backed chair with sheets of paper scattered around her like molting feathers.

No wonder she was eager to have him buy back the goldfinch. No doubt she had spent money on it she shouldn't have and was eager to get it back so they could hire a maid or maybe buy a new dress.

"Gran," she called to the elderly woman, "we have company."

"How lovely." The woman never looked up from her sketch. "He might find a clear seat. And if you bring him some lemonade, will you get me some, too?"

Daire nearly gasped in shock that she didn't want to know his name, what he was doing there, what connection brought him to their house. That the children seemed uninterested in his arrival wasn't surprising, but a grandmother should show more curiosity or concern for the company her granddaughter kept.

"Would you like some?" Miss Morris asked him.

Afraid if he said no the grandmother wouldn't get hers, Daire nodded. "Thank you. It is a warm day."

He hoped the glass was clean.

"I'll fetch that then get your bottle." She darted from the room, pausing in the doorway long enough to say, "Do sit down."

Not certain which chair to clear of baby paraphernalia, books, or dolls, Daire remained standing. "Would you like me to pick up your drawings for you, ma'am?"

"That would be kind of you, young man." Gran dropped another sketch onto the pile.

Daire stooped to gather them up. He didn't know what he expected to see, a still life, perhaps, or nice landscapes, the sort of thing females usually drew. But this lady was a caricature artist. When he saw the most recent one to land on the floor showed him cringing away from an oversized glass of liquid, he laughed aloud.

She might look indifferent hunched over her tablet, but she was an observant old lady.

"Nice." She gave him an approving glance from beneath bushy eyebrows. "Susan is the only one in my family who ever laughs at my drawings."

"I come from a family of artists." Daire stacked the drawings into a neat heap. "I know talent when I see it."

"Wish one of my grandchildren got it. The older girls don't care for drawing, and Susan couldn't draw flies."

Daire flinched at the unkindness. He sought for something

complimentary to say about her to counteract the bluntness. "She's very pretty."

"Not compared to her sisters. Susan is our ugly duckling who isn't going to turn into a swan."

Daire was glad to hear footfalls heading toward the parlor so he didn't have to respond. Contradicting his elders wasn't proper, but he wanted to. Susan might not be likely to turn into a graceful swan, but ugly she was not.

She strode into the room bearing two glasses of lemonade. The glasses looked clean, and their fine quality surprised him considering the shabbiness of the house.

He rose and went to greet her. "Thank you." The beverage was cool, and his mouth watered for the refreshment of sweetened lemon. "But none for you?"

"I'll serve some to the children after you go." She swept past him, her face so stony he wondered if she'd overheard her grandmother's remark. "Here you go, Gran. Where's Bridget?"

Gran shrugged. "Haven't seen her all day. But take care of this fine young man and just ignore me."

"We could never ignore you, Gran." The smile she gave her grandmother lit her face to loveliness an artist like the old lady should notice. "I think Mr. Grassick will only be here for a few more minutes." She glanced around then darted over to a chair and gathered up the pile of magazines sliding across the cushion. "Do sit down, sir. I'll fetch the goldfinch."

Before Daire could respond with something polite, she dashed off through the doorway again. Her footfalls rang on the floorboards then died abruptly, likely reaching a rug. Silence stretched for several moments, broken only by the distant yelling of the children and the nearby scratch of the grandmother's pencil.

A sudden crash sent Daire charging from the parlor, lemonade splashing out of his glass and over his hand. "Miss Morris?"

"In here." Her voice sounded odd, thick.

Daire's heart stopped. He envisioned her standing amid shards of broken yellow glass. Instead, he found her standing in the dining room amid broken glass, but it was clear, having covered the faces of several photographs that now lay with the glass at her feet.

"It's gone," she wailed, flinging her hands up to her face. "I am so sorry, Mr. Grassick, but your goldfinch bottle is missing."

four

Anger flashed in Daire Grassick's green eyes—anger and something more Susan couldn't name. Disgust perhaps, or disdain. And no wonder. She'd lost a valuable piece of artwork and hadn't noticed it was gone. With the chaos of the house, no wonder she hadn't missed the object.

Looking away from the aversion tightening his face, Susan became aware of her bedraggled dress, her loose hair, and the bread crumbs on the dining room carpet. No one took care of the house as well as they should, including her. Their only maid came and went as she pleased, her two eldest sisters—Daisy and Opal—were off to their own homes, and Momma and Deborah simply didn't care about housework. That left the household management to Susan, and she wasn't any better with it than she was with sewing or drawing.

Maybe the bank manager would let her use her inheritance to hire a maid. Not that that would help now with the pictures on the floor where she'd knocked them in her frantic search for the goldfinch bottle. She heard the children coming toward the back door and realized she needed to clean up the glass immediately before the younger ones crawled into it and hurt themselves.

"I'm so sorry." She dropped to her knees and began to gather up the shards of broken glass.

At least she could pay to replace the damaged frames.

"I set it on the mantel here the day I got it from you," she babbled on. "No one liked it. They thought I spent my money foolishly. So I stuck it behind the frame. Then I tried to sell it on Monday, but no one wanted to buy it. And I put it back here. I know I put it back here."

"Are you certain you didn't put it on a different mantel?" Mr. Grassick's voice, though quiet, resonated through the room like a bell tolling her doom. "Like the parlor or a sitting room or even the kitchen?"

"No, not the kitchen. I'm as bad at cooking as I am—" She realized she was talking too much and concentrated for a few moments on clearing the carpet of glass and a number of other things that shouldn't have been there, such as the silver button from a child's coat and a teaspoon, and dumping them into her lap.

"Perhaps I should go look in the parlor," Mr. Grassick suggested. "The mantel looked. . .crowded."

"All right. Do so." Susan popped her finger in her mouth to remove a fleck of blood obtained from a sliver of glass. "Gran won't care. But be careful of the toys on the floor."

"Don't you all have a nursery?" His tone held more curiosity than censure—she hoped.

She glanced up at him through the curtain of her hair. "We do, but it's at the top of the house and is only large enough for two children. So when all of them are here like today, we keep them downstairs."

"And the weather is too fine to confine them to an upstairs room." Daire started to smile.

A shriek from the backyard wiped the smile from his face and sent her surging to her feet. Glass sprinkled from her skirt in a ringing cascade. "I should never have left them alone." She charged for the door.

The kitchen door stood open, allowing a swarm of flies to swoop around the room, but giving her clear access to the garden and children. All of them huddled near the lilac bushes, some talking, some standing still, their thumbs in their mouths, others crying.

One bellowed the loudest, a toddler from the sound of it. Unable to see who it was for certain, through the phalanx of children, Susan began picking them up and moving them aside.

"Let me by." She reached Paul and dropped a hand onto his shoulder. "Who is it?"

"Jerald." Paul stepped aside.

The youngest of the nephews huddled on the ground, a bunch of lilacs crushed in one hand, his face as red as beet juice. Wails loud enough to awaken a sleeping Australian in Sydney pierced the afternoon.

Resisting the urge to cover her ears, Susan dropped to her knees beside the baby and tried to pick him up. If possible, he bellowed louder.

"What happened?" she shouted to the others.

"We don't know," Paul yelled back. "We were playing tag, and he started crying."

"I suppose no one was watching him?" The flash of anger sharpening her voice lent more to distress with herself than with the children's neglect.

She'd been so thrilled to have Daire Grassick find her, she hadn't thought for a moment about leaving the children unattended. They were in the yard after all, and Roger was old enough to be responsible.

Except Roger wasn't there.

"Where's your brother?" she asked Paul.

He shrugged, his thin shoulder feeling like a bag of bones beneath her hand. "He said he was going to get some water and never came back."

"He didn't come into the house."

So she'd lost track of Sam and Roger, all for Daire Grassick, who had only gone to the trouble of tracking her down so he could get his silly bottle back. And she couldn't return it to him, let alone sell it back to him. It was missing, and now she had a mess in the dining room, a ruined dress, and most definitely nothing that would make the handsome stranger want to stay a moment longer than it took to find his artwork.

With a bit of regret that she couldn't curl up on the grass and wail like her nephew, Susan tried to pick him up again.

When she touched his chubby little arm, his scream sounded as though she had just taken a hacksaw to the limb. She recoiled and did start to cry, though silently.

"Let me." A shadow fell across the scene, then Daire Grassick crouched beside her.

He reached for Jerald, too, but made no attempt to pick him up. Instead, he cradled the boy's hand in his own long, strong fingers and touched the exposed skin just above the baby's wrist. With a flick of his fingers, he seemed to stop the yowling. At least Jerald stopped crying more than a few hiccuping sobs, and he gazed up at Mr. Grassick with huge blue eyes full of wonder.

Susan gazed at him with wonder, too. "What did you do?"

Behind them, the children murmured in tones of awe.

Mr. Grassick shrugged. "I removed a stinger from a bee." He gestured to the flowering bushes. "They're all over, and he was clutching some of the flowers."

"And you found the stinger." Susan reached for her nephew.

This time, Jerald flung himself into her arms and clung to her neck.

"Come into the house, baby." She tried to stand, but her feet caught in the ragged hem of her skirt, and she swayed to one side, bumping into a nearby child.

A scene of her and the children tumbling onto the grass like pieces in a game of dominoes flashed through her mind. But she couldn't catch herself without dropping Jerald.

Daire Grassick snatched the baby from her. With her hands free, she caught her balance and scrambled to her feet. She didn't want to look at the gentleman, afraid of what his expression would be this time.

A snort drew her attention anyway. Instead of the disgust she expected, his eyes danced and his lips twitched. He coughed, but one of the children giggled, then another and another, and Daire Grassick joined in the hilarity.

Wordlessly, Susan took Jerald from his arms and headed

for the house. Now that Mr. Grassick had removed the stinger, she saw the spot on the baby's wrist, a small red welt.

"We'll take care of that in a minute, sweetie." She held her nephew close. "Then I'll give you a cracker."

"We're hungry, too," the other children chorused.

"I expect you are." Susan gave Daire Grassick a helpless glance. "I'm sorry, but I should feed the children."

"I'll help. It might get done faster." His dry tone matched the resigned expression on his face.

Susan winced. "I'm sorry. Why don't you let me know where you're staying? I'll look for the goldfinch after I get the little ones down for a nap. When I find it, I'll get word to you."

"I'll help," he repeated. To Susan's astonishment, he hefted the other two toddlers into his arms and headed for the kitchen door.

"Come along, everyone." Susan addressed the rest of the throng. "There's bread and cheese and lemonade."

And Mr. Grassick was going to regret the day she'd caught sight of the goldfinch bottle from the corner of her eye and stopped to admire it. But he'd seemed desperate to sell it then. Now he looked anything but desperate. His clothes were impeccable, his hair was trimmed with a perfect crest above the brow, and he smelled of sandalwood. If he'd been poor a week ago, his fortunes had changed drastically.

Maybe he was a gambler. The notion made Susan shudder with revulsion. Then annoyance tightened her lips. If so, his disdain of their chaotic house was unfounded.

If he wasn't, the shabbiness of the house was embarrassing, not to mention her appearance. She must look like a ragamuffin from the street instead of a young lady who had inherited a small fortune from her great-aunt. Probably most of his dislike of his surroundings focused on her.

Susan wanted to crawl under the kitchen table or maybe even descend to the cellar until Mr. Grassick left. She knew after they located the goldfinch bottle she would never see him again, so her appearance didn't matter. But if this was an example of how matters would lie if she managed to have another gentleman call on her, whatever the reason, she would end up an old maid. She couldn't think how her brothers-in-law had wanted to marry into such a haphazard family. But then, her sisters were intelligent and beautiful, talented and friendly—everything Susan was not. At least she wasn't in comparison to them.

Unable to hide away with all the children to feed and half of them to put down for a rest, Susan entered the kitchen and set about slicing bread from an array of loaves someone had either baked or purchased. Daire Grassick joined her at the worktable and commenced slicing off hunks of cheese to lay atop the bread. Paul, bless him, distributed the food to the rest of the group then poured lemonade. At last, the noise settled down as everyone ate. Susan's stomach growled, but she wasn't about to take a bite in front of Mr. Grassick. She feared she would end up with bread crumbs down her front and cheese smeared on her upper lip.

"Would you like something to eat?" she asked him.

"No, thank you. I'd rather get on with things." He glanced at the mantel. It jutted out over the stove, since they had installed that instead of using the fireplace for cooking many years earlier. Pots and pans rested atop the mantel, along with a spoon that belonged with the dirty dishes.

Susan snatched it up and dumped it into the sink with the plates from someone else's meal. "It's not there, either."

"No." Mr. Grassick looked at the table and children devouring their food. "Should we take something to your grandmother?"

"Oh, goodness, yes." Susan closed her eyes.

How could she have forgotten Gran?

"She'll just want some butter on her bread, no cheese."

"I want butter and no cheese," one of the children cried.

"You eat your cheese." Susan gave the girl a stern glance. "You need to grow big and strong. Paul, will you take this to Gran?"

"I'll take it." Daire took the plate from her hands. "And I'll look for the goldfinch in there."

"Thank you. That's very kind of you." Susan picked a piece of soggy bread off the floor from beneath Jerald's chair. "No, baby, you have to eat this. See, I gave you only the soft part."

When she straightened, Daire had vanished. She wanted to pray that he would find his family treasure. But prayers were for people like her mother and sisters, those who did good work and God noticed. Still, she found her heart yearning for a good outcome. Otherwise—

"It's not here." Daire returned bearing a glass of milk that reeked from all the way across the room.

"Ugh." Susan wrinkled her nose and wished she could hide her face. "Who left that there?"

"It hardly matters." Daire carried the glass outside then returned in a moment to set the empty glass with the other dishes. "I didn't see the goldfinch anywhere."

"I am so sorry."

More than he could know. She was used to her chaotic home, and although she didn't like it, it was familiar. Seen through the eyes of this well-dressed and handsome stranger, the flaws of her surroundings glared like sunlight on tin. The sooner he left, the sooner she could stop being ashamed of her house and family—and herself.

"Let me get the babies down for a nap, and I'll look elsewhere." She glanced around at the older children who would never agree to resting. "Will you play outside again or take a book and read? I need you all to be a bit quieter so the babies will sleep. Mr. Grassick, maybe you should come back later or—or meet us at church tomorrow."

Daire said nothing but looked pensive. The older children filed around him like a stream dividing around a rock. They slipped outside, as she knew they would do, rather than read with Gran in the parlor.

"Mr. Grassick?" Susan arched one brow at him.

He shook his head. "Perhaps that would be best. Which church?"

She told him.

"I'll be there. No need to see me out." Unsmiling, he left the kitchen. His footfalls echoed on the hall floor; then the front door clicked shut.

Although the children had begun another boisterous game outside and the two youngest toddlers were beginning to whimper from fatigue, the house felt empty, barren of light.

Heart heavy, Susan picked up Jerald and called to the others to follow her into her mother's sitting room across from the big parlor. It was cool and dark with its curtains drawn. She laid them in a row atop a blanket on the rug and covered them with another blanket.

"Sleep well, little ones." She gave them each a kiss. "I'll stay here until you fall asleep."

She spent the next moments searching for the goldfinch. She couldn't imagine any way in which the object could have found its way into the sitting room, but she didn't know how it would have gotten out of the dining room, either.

Thinking of the dining room, she recalled her need to clear away the broken glass. Once the babies slept, she left for the other room. But the glass had been cleared away and the frames set back on the mantel. The sound of clattering dishes in the kitchen drew her into that chamber. Bridget stood at the sink, scrubbing plates.

"Where were you?" Susan asked.

"Shopping." Bridget pointed her sharp chin toward the table.

Several baskets of foodstuffs sat there.

"We were out of nearly everything," she continued. "I don't know when anyone did the shopping last, and with all these little ones here, there wasn't a thing left."

"No, I suppose I should have gone. Momma's so busy." Susan began to unpack the baskets. "Bridget, have you seen that goldfinch bottle I brought home last Friday?"

"Not today." Bridget dipped water from the reservoir behind the stove and poured it over the dishes to rinse them. "Weren't it on the mantel in the dining room?"

"Yes, behind Daisy's wedding picture." Susan stood gazing at a wrapped sugar loaf as though she could read an answer on the plain white paper. "But it's not there now."

"I've got to get supper started, or I'd be helping you." Bridget took the loaf from Susan and carried it to the pantry. "I'll watch the children so you can look."

"Thank you."

Susan looked. She hunted behind cushions and under chairs, atop mantels and inside cupboards. The only room she didn't inspect was the one belonging to her parents. She wouldn't invade their privacy. Besides that, she couldn't believe they would have it there. Momma had been so opposed to the bottle, she wouldn't want it around as a reminder of her daughter's foolishness, and Daddy had never known of its existence.

At last, Susan admitted defeat. She stood in the middle of the parlor, watching Gran draw something more detailed than usual, and wondered how she would face Mr. Daire Grassick in the morning. The temptation to remain with the little ones and send a message through one of her brothers ran high. But she'd agreed to meet him there; thus, for the first time in at least a year, perhaps longer if she thought about the exact date, she was going to attend an actual church service—because of Daire Grassick.

five

Daire heaved a sigh of relief as the front gate banged shut behind him. Although children played in other gardens and a chorus of birds serenaded the neighborhood from the tops of tall oaks and maples lining the street, compared to the Morris household, the rest of the world lay in stillness and neat array.

As he traversed the brick walkway back to the harbor and his hotel, he thanked God for his own home. Nothing ever went missing in his family until the secret formula for the Balmoral crystal. Grandma and Momma kept the household running as smoothly as Grandpa and his brother ran the glassworks, and Father, the farm. He'd mislaid himself for a while, but no more. His family wanted him back and, as soon as he returned the goldfinch and formula to the household from which he'd taken it, he would rejoin them and start to make himself useful.

But he would never achieve his goal if he depended on Susan Morris.

At the end of the block, he glanced back at her home. He doubted they were poor. The house was large amid other fine homes that signaled prosperity. Yet everything appeared neglected, including Susan herself.

Thought of the bedraggled young woman, apparently overwhelmed by too many children to look after and his arrival, sent his heart twisting with pity, frustration, or attraction, or perhaps all three. Her care for her grandmother and children, whatever their relationship to her—brothers and sisters or nieces and nephews—struck a chord of approval inside Daire, to whom his family had once again become all important. Her prettiness beneath the bedraggled hair and gown added to

51

her appeal for him. And that jolt when she'd brushed the lilac petals from his sleeve—

"No, not again." He spoke aloud to make the words more important, more definite.

A passerby glanced in his direction then ducked his head and hastened past.

Daire grinned. Living in the country most of his life, where he often saw no one on his long walks or afternoons fishing, he'd gotten used to giving himself an audible talking-to without worrying what others thought. There in Hudson City, he'd broken himself of the habit, but a few days back in Salem County had changed all that. He'd spent hours walking through the fields and woods, absorbing the peace and serenity of his surroundings and the joy of knowing he had a fine home and loving family to return to.

Until he went back into the parlor and saw the empty place on the mantel beneath Grandma's portrait, where Momma had set the goldfinch bottle when he was a child, declaring it was too special to the family to reside on her dressing table and hold perfume for her alone to enjoy.

"It's yours to give to your bride, Daire," she had told him. "Until then, it will sit here."

He'd taken it, believing he had found that bride—though his parents didn't approve—believing his future lay in the city, away from glass and farmland, neither of which had been his vocation. Her father was a customer of the glassworks. She came with him on a buying visit. One glance at her raven-haired beauty, and he'd believed every word she said about falling for him at first sight, about wanting a future together, about her faith in God.

"Stop thinking of that time." Daire paused to rest his hand on a streetlamp, welcoming its solidity, its steadiness. He let the cool metal anchor him in place like thoughts of his family.

He must go straight, not turn right, toward Lucinda's

house. His feet had taken him there so often, doing so now seemed natural, welcome. He wouldn't face an evening alone in the city. She would greet him with her warmth and smiles.

"I knew you'd come back," she would say as she had the first time he returned. "Daddy will be overjoyed to see you."

Daddy, with his questionable business practices; Daddy, who used his daughter to reel Daire into joining the Grassick name to the enterprise of luring young men into jobs out west, promising them riches in no time and good conditions in the meantime. He'd succeeded at first. Daire so wanted to make a fortune on his own, he invested all the money his father had given him for a stake in his future. Then, when Daire realized the business was dishonest, that the young men ended up working backbreaking labor for little food and low wages, he couldn't get the money back.

"Only if you stay," Lucinda told him. "That's what Daddy says."

He hadn't stayed, but when hunger took over because of his lack of income, he had returned to the temptation of Lucinda's adoration and beauty and constant searching after another form of revelry. With Lucinda came another future stake in the form of her dowry. He could have her, start his life anew, pay Father back—if he didn't think about the source of the money.

He'd thought about the source and grew weary of her flirtations. He'd thought of what his family had instilled in him as right and wrong and chose hunger once more until his pride in refusing to go home penniless compelled him to sell the goldfinch and the precious formula inside.

He hadn't chosen Susan as the person to whom he should sell it. She had approached him. Yet he couldn't help feeling as though he should have been wiser, started walking home, found a ride on a farm cart, even if it took him days to reach home—anything but sell the goldfinch to a lady who was careless with the possessions of others.

No, that wasn't fair to Susan. The goldfinch belonged to her. She had paid him well for the bauble. But she hadn't cared for it as a Grassick would.

Lucinda had been the same the one time he showed it to her. She made a careless remark about it being pretty then handed it back to him with such inattention she nearly dropped it on the maple floorboards, where it would have smashed to bits if Daire hadn't caught it.

Lucinda—careless with possessions, careless with hearts.

With evening falling on the city, others like her began to surround Daire. They spilled onto the sidewalks in their finery, girls too young to be out on their own and young men with faces already hardened by the world. Daire wanted to escape from the temptation of the city. He'd fallen back into it easily the first time and wasn't convinced his new resolve to remain worthy of his family's forgiveness would prove strong enough for him not to wish to mask his shame with noise and flirtations and. . .

He started walking again, his footfalls firm and determined to take him to his hotel. He would dine in his room and compose a letter for his family. Tomorrow he would meet Susan at her church, which was good. He didn't want to set foot inside the house again. The tumult reminded him too much of his life for the past six months. And he didn't like the guilt that had squeezed his insides at every turn. He needed order and answers, a sense that everything lay in its place, from his purpose in the world to his relationship with God.

Tomorrow all would be well and he could return home. Without doubt, Miss Susan Morris would have found the goldfinch by then. The house was chaotic, but surely no object the size of the perfume bottle would vanish completely, even in that mess.

&

Susan could never face Daire Grassick at church or anywhere else without the goldfinch bottle. She couldn't imagine why it was so important to him now, when a week ago he'd been anxious to get rid of it. But maybe his family had been upset with him over selling the family piece. He certainly looked distressed that the bottle was missing.

Its absence from the places she expected it to be distressed Susan. It emphasized the chaos of her home. How embarrassing to have him see such disarray. Finding his trinket would make up for him seeing her and her family at their worst.

As the children trickled inside, weary from play and seeking more food, she began to question them. "Have any of you seen a pretty yellow bird statue?" She glanced from the three eldest to the younger ones. "It's really a perfume bottle but stands about six inches high—"

"That silly thing you bought off some stranger?" Paul asked.

"Yes, have you seen it?" Susan leaned toward him, eager to have an answer.

"I saw it when Momma was showing it to Father and saying how silly you are," Paul said. "She wants you to support her missions not spend your money on toys."

"And she's right." Susan bit her lower lip and glanced at the other children.

No, none of them would know anything. They weren't tall enough to reach the mantel, though Opal's daughters were old enough to move a chair, stand on it, and reach anything on the shelf.

"I'll have to ask Momma when she gets home."

She paced to the parlor, where Gran sat reading instead of drawing. A pile of sketches lay on the floor beside her. Susan stooped to gather them up and glance through them. Several depicted children playing in a garden. Since Gran couldn't see the back lawn from her chair, Susan presumed Gran had drawn from imagination what she thought her grandchildren and great-grandchildren looked like playing outside.

"They're not nearly that gentle." Susan smiled at Gran. "Show the boys knocking one another down, and you have it."

"I like to think of them being kind to one another." Paper crackled as Gran turned the page of her book. "None of my great-grandchildren are mean."

"No, there's no meanness in them." Susan turned over another sheet. "This is precious."

Since Gran could see through the doorway to the sitting room, this must have come from observation. It showed three little heads poking from a blanket like puppets in a Punch and Judy show popping their heads up above a curtain.

Gran shrugged. "They're best when they're sleeping."

"That's—oh my." Susan caught her breath.

The next sketch in the pile showed Daire Grassick gazing at her. Rather than the contempt Susan believed he felt toward her, his dreamy eyes and half smile depicted wonder, as though. . . As though. . .

"As though he likes me." Susan felt warm all over, like when she drank a cup of hot chocolate.

"He's noticed you." Gran turned another page. "He didn't like me saying you're not pretty—that's for certain." She chuckled.

Susan winced in reaction to Gran saying she wasn't pretty. Yet if Daire Grassick didn't like it, he must think she was. And one of Gran's observant sketches said he'd noticed her, noticed her as a lady, not a flibbertigibbet.

Buoyed into further action on his behalf, Susan made another search of the house for the goldfinch. Not until she came up empty-handed did she think that, when she found it, he would be off to his family again. If they couldn't find it, he would likely be off to his family, anyway, and he would think less of her.

Susan was under no legal obligation to give or sell the goldfinch back to Daire Grassick, but she wanted to. She needed to have the purchase off her conscience. If the bottle was so important to him, he should have it at all costs. Once it was gone, if Daire Grassick vanished from her life, too, she would still be free to pursue a purpose for her life other than spending the inheritance her great-aunt had given her to catch herself a husband. She needed something special to take to a husband besides money so she knew he loved her first.

Daire Grassick would never love a female for money. He would prefer beauty and grace and poise and talent.

Could one buy poise and talent?

Susan pondered this notion as she rejoined the children. She was glad her sisters' children had spent the day with her. Opal and Daisy would have to come home with Momma and Deborah to collect the young ones, and Susan could ask them about the bottle then.

Father returned home first. Susan broke off in the middle of helping one of the girls put a new dress on her doll and ran up the steps after Father before he disappeared into his room.

"Have you seen that goldfinch bottle I bought last week?" she asked between gasps for air.

"Goldfinch bottle?" He gave her a befuddled look from his lavender blue eyes so like her own. "What is a goldfinch bottle?"

"It's a glass ornament, a perfume bottle, in the shape of a goldfinch taking off in flight. I bought it from Daire Grassick last week."

"Grassick." Father's face grew pensive. "Why do I know that name?"

"I don't know. I've never heard it before." She turned away. "But I really want to find that bottle again so I can get my money back."

"A goldfinch, you say?"

"Yes, a bottle shaped like one." Susan managed to keep the impatience from her tone, as the the familiar gleam brightened her father's eyes.

He was starting to compose a new poem.

"Fascinating." Father closed his eyes. "Sounds like a work of art."

"It is. Please. Have you seen it?"

"No, I haven't, but I'm sure I know the name Grassick. Tell me more about the bottle. It sounds interesting. Goldfinches are beautiful in the summer when their plumage changes color. Was this bottle yellow?"

"Yes, though more amber and made opaque to protect the perfume, except it was empty when I bought it. But surely you saw it." She grasped his arm. "It was on the mantel in the dining room."

"Nothing but wedding pictures on that mantel. Used to be a painting there before the girls insisted they needed photographs." He grimaced. "No poetry in those stiff poses." He patted her hand. "And that reminds me. Thank you for the notebooks. That's the sort of thing to be buying, not some bottle shaped like a bird."

"I know it was foolish of me." Susan removed her hand from his arm and clutched her fingers together behind her back. "I saw it and had the money and. . ."

The man holding it had caught her attention as much as the ornament had.

"Never you mind, Father. I want to sell it back to the young man I bought it from, but I can't find it."

"Not surprising you've misplaced something. I lost a book of my poems last night."

"Oh, no, do you need me to help you find it?"

"No, child, thank you." He smiled, making his eyes go dreamy. "I found it inside my Bible. Just shows reading your Bible every day is good for you." Chuckling as though he'd made a great joke, he patted her cheek and slipped into the suite of rooms he shared with Momma.

Stabbed with guilt that her Bible lay collecting dust on her bedside table, Susan returned to the children playing in the parlor. Silence on the other side of the door sent the hairs on the back of her neck rising as though brushed by a frosty hand. No way should a room holding Gran and more than half a dozen children be that quiet.

Heart thumping like a fleeing rabbit, she pushed open the door and shrieked. A red substance like blood covered the face of nearly every child and the hands of most. Red also appeared on cushions and the carpet beside an overturned jar of raspberry preserves that hadn't been set down properly.

"Where did you get that?" Relief sharpened her tone.

"The look on your face." Gran's rusty laugh scraped through the room. "Did you think someone was stabbed?"

"Several of them." Heart still running away inside her chest, Susan skewered Paul. "Did Bridget get that down for you?"

"We wanted something sweet, and Bridget and you weren't around." He looked sullen. "I tried to spread it on bread, but it was too watery, so we just got spoons."

"Then I suggest you go get a bucket of water and several rags." Susan glanced at the rug. "And Bridget with some soda."

Paul jumped to his feet and raced for the door. The instant the clatter of his footfalls diminished, Susan understood the reason for his haste to obey her.

Momma and the sisters were coming up the front walk.

Susan groaned. "I shouldn't have left them alone for even a minute."

The first time that day she'd left the children unattended, Jerald had gotten stung by a bee. This second time, clothes, cushions, and carpet had likely gotten ruined. And all for the same reason.

Susan wished she could run away for the day like the two eldest of her brothers had. But she stood to face the women in her family. She had forgotten about her own bedraggled appearance until they swept into the parlor on a wave of floral scents and rustling skirts and all four of them stopped to goggle at her.

"What happened to your hair?" Deborah asked.

"And your dress?" Opal added. "I liked that dress. What did you do to ruin it?"

"It's a long story." Susan took a deep breath. "We have a bit of a mess with the children—"

Opal spotted her offspring and exclaimed in horror at the same time Momma cried out over the carpet.

"How did this happen?" Momma demanded of Susan.

"I was talking to Father. . . ." She shook her head. "It has to do with that goldfinch bottle I bought. Have any of you seen it?"

They stared at her.

"The children, you, and this room are a mess," Momma said, her lips tight, "and you're asking about that bit of frivolity you wasted your money on?"

"None of this would have happened if the goldfinch was where I left it." Afraid her response sounded disrespectful, she bowed her head. "The young man I bought it from found me and wanted to buy it back, but I can't find it anywhere. Mr. Grassick and I were looking for it when Jerald got stung—"

With a wail of horror, Daisy swooped down on her baby and scooped him up, raspberry jam and all. Momma tapped her fan against her chin, murmuring, "Grassick," as though she, too, thought she should know the name. Then Paul and Bridget returned with buckets of water, soap, rags, and soda, and the cleanup process began.

An hour later, with the parlor damp but fairly clean, perhaps cleaner that it had been before, and the children bundled off to their homes, Susan found time to mend her own appearance. She finished changing her gown and pinning up her hair in time to join Momma, Deborah, and Daddy for dinner. From the cacophony in the kitchen, the older boys had returned home and decided to eat in there, as usual.

Once she sat across from Momma at one end of the long dining table, Susan wished she could dine with Bridget supervising the meal instead of Momma. She and Daddy cast disapproving glances in Susan's direction but said little directly to her. Susan picked at her food and said nothing. The conversation revolved around Deborah and her plans to go with her longtime beau, Gerrit Vandervoort, to a hymn-singing at church that night.

"It'll be the last time I let him court me if he doesn't propose on the way home." Deborah pouted. "He's been courting me for three years, so no other man at church will court me, but he won't ask me to marry him either."

"He hasn't asked my permission to make you an offer," Father admitted.

"Then you're right not to court him." Momma nodded. "Don't even let him sit near us in church tomorrow. Let everyone know you've jilted him instead of the other way around."

"Oh, indeed I shall." Deborah's blue eyes gleamed.

Susan pitied Gerrit. He didn't have a chance, and maybe he shouldn't. He wasn't being fair to Deborah, staking a claim on her but never offering marriage. And maybe if Deborah were safely wed and out of the house, Momma would notice Susan was unmarried and without so much as a beau.

Thoughts of courting and beaux led Susan back to Daire Grassick and the goldfinch bottle. She racked her brain to figure out where the goldfinch could have gone. She determined to find it. Until she did, she couldn't justify the disasters of the day or redeem her poor decision in purchasing the object in the first place. Once she had her money back, she would find something to spend it on that would give her a purpose in her life, a way to make her family happy with, if not proud of, her.

When Deborah came home later, still without an engagement, she gained everyone's attention by bursting into tears the instant the front door closed behind her. "He brought his stepmother's younger sister along with his little sister."

Her wails were loud enough for Gerrit to hear them from his house three blocks away. "She's only eighteen and so very pretty."

"No one's prettier than you," Susan said with all sincerity.

"Nell is." Deborah yanked the hat from her head and tossed it onto the table. "Her hat was brand-new, and I've worn this at least three times."

"You're frugal with your allowance." Momma hugged Deborah so she had a shoulder to cry on. "You care more for those less fortunate than frivolities." Momma shot Susan a glare.

"You can wear my new hat tomorrow," Susan offered.

It wasn't generous of her; she could buy a new one in a minute.

Deborah stopped crying long enough to smile at Susan. "That's very sweet of you, Sue, but that shade of pink is too dark for my coloring."

"Then I'll get you a new hat on Monday." Susan knew just the one.

"Silly of Aunt Susan to give you her money." Father shook his head. "If Deborah had a fortune like that, Gerrit would marry her."

"Then I wouldn't want him." Deborah straightened and wiped her eyes. "If he can't take me in an old hat and without a fortune, then I'll let everyone know I'm not spoken for."

Back straight, she marched upstairs.

Neither parent looked happy.

They weren't any happier the next morning than the night before. Deborah's eyes were red rimmed and Susan spent so much time locating, then needing to iron a gown that matched her new hat, that she ended up running downstairs and out the front door as the others were leaving the gate.

"You should have been there already to help with the children," Momma said.

"I'm not helping with the children this morning." Susan

twisted her gloved hands in the cords of her reticule. "Mr. Grassick is meeting me at the church to learn if I found his goldfinch bottle."

"Mr. Grassick?" Momma and Daddy both gave Susan their full attention.

"Is he related to the Grassick Glassworks?" Daddy asked. "I remembered where I heard the name."

"I—I don't know." Susan stumbled over a bit of rough pavement. "I've never heard of the glassworks."

"You drink out of tumblers they make nearly every meal," Momma said. "They—Paul, Roger, don't run ahead of us."

The boys slowed but remained a dozen yards ahead.

Momma drew her brows together for a moment then continued. "They've been making glass down in Salem County for over fifty years. Very successful."

"They had a display at the Great Exhibition in London seven years ago," Deborah added. "Now they make glass for the queen."

"Then I wonder why he would have had to sell a piece of glass to get enough money to get home," Susan mused aloud.

"The city has many ways to steal money from the unwary." Daddy gave Susan a pointed glance.

She winced. "Yes, I know. I shouldn't have bought it. But I'm puzzled. Why would one little piece of glass be so important to him if his family makes glass?"

"Whatever the reason," Momma said, "we need to get it back to him as soon as possible. You said he was meeting us here?" Her gaze traveled across the lawn of the church, where several people gathered beneath the spreading branches of an oak to shade themselves from the late spring sunshine.

One man stood on the church steps engaged in conversation with the pastor. At the sight of his tall, broad frame, Susan felt as though her insides had turned the consistency of the badly set jelly on the parlor rug. She had nothing to tell him. She'd questioned every member of her family, and none had known a bit of the goldfinch's whereabouts. Perhaps she should ask them again, take the children aside one by one to see if maybe one of them had taken the trinket and now feared the consequences of their action.

She glanced around, letting her gaze gather the scattered members of her family. They were all there—her two eldest sisters, their husbands, and their children. Momma and Daddy and Deborah with her, as well as—

She stopped so abruptly her hoops swayed as though a high wind blew across the lawn. "Momma, Daddy, where's Sam?"

Momma halted. "What do you mean where's Sam? He's—" The crease between her brows appeared again, and she turned to Daddy. "Have you seen Sam this morning?"

"I haven't seen him since yesterday morning," Father admitted. "Ask the boys."

As discreetly as possible in a crowd, Momma called Roger and Paul to her side and asked about Sam. They shrugged in response.

"He was around yesterday morning," Paul said. "I know, because he was talking about playing some game where you hit the ball with sticks like cricket but more fun."

"I saw him on Market Street yesterday afternoon," Roger said. "We'd been down to the docks to see a clipper from China; then we had an ice cream and I came home. He said he'd be along later."

"Maybe he went to Opal's or Daisy's." Noting that Daire had spotted her and was headed her way, Susan hastened to catch up with her sisters and ask about their eldest brother, sixteen-year-old Sam. By the time she reached Opal, Daire had caught up with her.

"Did you lose something else?" he asked, one dark brow arched, the corners of his mouth twitching.

Susan wanted to snap that this was no joke. But she merely nodded and gave a brief explanation. "No one has seen our brother Samuel since yesterday afternoon. We all thought he was with someone else. But no one's seen him."

"I see." His lips stopped twitching. His eyes narrowed, intensifying the brilliant green. "The goldfinch bottle and your brother have both gone missing from your household without anyone noticing for at least a day. Very peculiar."

"Yes, it's—" Susan stopped as his words sunk in. Understanding of the meaning behind his words knotted her stomach, and she grew aware of the staring faces, the lull in the conversations around them. Nonetheless, she had to ask him what he suggested, just to make certain. "Are you hinting that my brother stole the goldfinch?"

six

Daire thought he should shrivel under Susan's glare. Although their looks were vastly different, Daire recognized his sister Maggie in Susan's fierce expression, her challenging demand to know if he was maligning a member of her family. Maggie was like that—defending every one of them whether they deserved it or not. And gazing into Susan's lovely wisteria-colored eyes, he felt something inside him give way, a thrilling twist in the middle like swooping over rapids on a raft.

"I'm sorry." He took her hand in both of his and applied just a bit of pressure. "I guess that didn't come out well."

Falling for another city female wouldn't come out well either, and for that he was sorrier than making an accusation against one of the Morris clan.

"Of course Mr. Grassick wouldn't mean anything so rude as to accuse Samuel of theft." A middle-aged beauty smiled up at him. "You are Daire Grassick, are you not?"

"Yes, ma'am." Daire released Susan's hand.

"This is my mother, Mrs. Morris," Susan said. Her face was flushed, her eyes veiled behind their gold-tipped lashes. "And this is the rest of them." She gestured to the growing crowd, all the sisters looking like their mother, the two brothers and Susan taking after the father. "Except for the eldest boy, Samuel. He's. . .missing, like your goldfinch."

"It's your goldfinch, Miss Morris." Daire still cringed at having so much as hinted at an accusation against a young man he didn't even know. "You purchased it from me quite honestly."

"And a foolish waste of her money it was." Mrs. Morris

66

shook her head and bestowed an indulgent glance on her youngest daughter. "But I suppose we should send some people out to hunt for Samuel. He's probably sound asleep in his bed. William, Marcus?" She directed her attention to her two sons-in-law. "Will you go see if you can find Samuel? If he's not in bed, he'll be playing ball in the park."

"How old is your brother?" Daire asked Susan in an undertone.

"Sixteen." She drew her brows together over her tip-tilted nose. "He's usually more responsible about his disappearances."

"He's done this before?" Daire couldn't keep the astonishment from his voice. "And no one sees that he is with the family?"

"Someone always thinks he's with someone else." Susan looked from her sisters' husbands to her parents, to her younger brothers, and finally to Deborah, who couldn't take her eyes off Daire, before giving him a sidelong glance. "You've seen my house. You can understand how one of us could go missing. One time I—" She snapped her teeth together, biting off her words, as her cheeks turned a darker pink than the ribbons on her bonnet. "Samuel can take care of himself."

"In the city at sixteen?" Daire clamped his own teeth against saying more.

He knew better. The world offered too many temptations for young men on their own, and the city magnified them by having all the lures so close together.

"I'll be happy to go looking for him," Daire finished instead.

"That's so kind of you to offer." Mrs. Morris turned back to him and touched his arm. "My sons-in-law will find him. They always have in the past. And we'll find your trinket, too. Right now, it's time for the service. Susan, take your father's arm."

"Maybe I should help look for Sam, too," Susan murmured.

"Nonsense." Mrs. Morris laughed. "Why ever would you skip services for something the men can do better, when we have a guest? You will be our guest, will you not, Mr. Grassick? We all have dinner together after church, and you're more than welcome."

"Thank you." He glanced at Susan for a clue as to why her family was so friendly to him.

Another sister, Deborah, caught his eye instead and smiled. He nodded then turned toward Susan.

She kept her face averted just enough that the brim of her rather fetching hat hid her expression, and she drew back into the throng of her family, edging to the outskirts with the married siblings and their offspring.

"I'd like to hear more about this goldfinch object." Miss Deborah Morris fell into step beside Daire as the lot of them headed for the church doors. "I've seen other *objets d'art* of the Grassick Glassworks, but never a goldfinch."

Understanding dawned. He wasn't really a stranger. At least his family name was familiar to Susan's parents and at least one sibling. They knew the Grassick Glassworks and thus probably something of the family, which included him, an excellent catch for their unmarried daughters.

"The goldfinch is special," Daire answered Miss Deborah. "I should never have sold it."

If he'd known what lay inside, he'd never have taken it. No, Maggie shouldn't have left the formula inside the goldfinch, but his need to impress Lucinda had done the damage.

Lucinda's face flashed across his mind's eye. He shouldn't have been without money. Until he'd refused to work further with her father, he'd been a good catch for her, too. Her father had brought her to Salem County deliberately to meet him. Lucinda's family had appeared just as qualified for an alliance—prosperous and warm. Daire ignored his father's warnings about their lack of adherence to their spiritual lives. Church, to Lucinda, was for socializing and for business connections for her father.

In his brief talk with the pastor before the Morrises arrived,

Daire discovered a man of deep convictions who expected his congregation came to grow in their relationship with the Lord, not show off their newest gowns or walking sticks. That lay in the Morrises' favor. Coupled with a family so careless with their possessions that a missing son didn't raise alarm, however, Daire didn't think they were a family with whom he would like to ally himself.

"Is there a story behind this goldfinch?" Mrs. Morris asked. "It seems an odd object to be so valuable to the family."

"Yes, I agree that it's odd." Daire smiled over memory of the story often told in the family. "It was my grandfather's betrothal gift to my grandmother in 1809. Grandfather won't allow any more of them to be made in our glasshouse."

"A betrothal gift." Miss Deborah fairly cooed. "So sweet and romantic." She gave him a melting glance from beneath the brim of her flower-bedecked hat.

Across the porch, a man of about his own age glared at him with a sharpness that should have sliced the buttons off Daire's coat then gave Deborah the same look. The message was clear—the other man didn't like Deborah with Daire.

Deborah stepped a bit closer to him, her hand curving around his forearm. "How did you manage to find our little house to buy back your trinket?"

"I asked around the shops with Miss Susan's description until I found someone who knew where she lived."

Daire couldn't even see where Susan was at that moment between Morrises, hats, and the scowling man.

"I never imagined she wouldn't still have it," he added.

If they hadn't reached the door of the church at that moment, he would have made a hasty exit. But exiting meant giving up hope of finding the goldfinch, and that meant returning home empty-handed. Going home empty-handed once had been bad enough. Now that he knew the consequences of doing so, he wouldn't do so again. He couldn't watch his family ruined.

He endured the second youngest Morris daughter's attention,

the glowers from the stranger, and numerous curious glances until they reached the sanctuary. The Morrises took up three pews because of the large number of children and the ladies' voluminous skirts. Daire found himself wedged between two pairs of hoops—Deborah's and Susan's. All through the service, which was truly excellent, he found himself watching Susan instead of paying as much attention to the sermon as he should have been. She kept her gaze either toward the pastor or choir or down at her hymnal or Bible. He didn't catch so much as a sidelong glance from her. She seemed intent on the service, singing softly but in a voice as pure and sweet as he would expect an angel's to sound. Around them, the other Morrises sang in a less tuneful manner. Music, apparently, was not a talent the Morrises shared with Susan.

Once the sermon began, she sat twisting her hands in her lap so hard he expected the seams of her gloves to split open. Once he caught the toe of her shoe tapping against the floor. Several times she glanced to the pastor then toward the window.

Daire wondered if she disliked the message. It was good, solid teaching but not convicting to a person whose heart was right with the Lord. Of course, hers might not be.

Or perhaps she was simply distressed about her brother. He would be. He wouldn't sit still in a service not knowing where a member of his family had gone. He knew his family had been praying for him over the last six months and hadn't come after him because he'd insisted on being on his own, and they understood dragging him back would accomplish nothing for the stubborn and wayward heart. But he was a man of five and twenty. Samuel was a boy of sixteen, far too young to be on his own for a day.

Daire wanted to take Susan's hand and leave the church so they could begin the hunt. Foolishness. The family knew their own. The boy was merely playing or sleeping. They should have noticed he was gone, and maybe this was a lesson to them to take more care in the future.

"What man of you," the pastor read from the fifteenth chapter of Luke, "having an hundred sheep, if he lose one of them, doth not leave the ninety and nine in the wilderness, and go after that which is lost, until he find it? And when he hath found it, he layeth it on his shoulders, rejoicing. And when he cometh home, he calleth together his friends and neighbours, saying unto them, Rejoice with me; for I have found my sheep which was lost. I say unto you, that likewise joy shall be in heaven over one sinner that repenteth, more than over ninety and nine just persons, which need no repentance."

Daire smiled, taking comfort in the words. He was the lost sheep who had gotten home. His family had rejoiced. They would rejoice again when he got back to Salem County. But he couldn't feel redeemed yet. He'd let them down and must make sure he deserved to go back with his soul spotless once more. Finding the precious formula would accomplish that.

Beside him, Susan shifted and twisted her hands and glanced toward the stained-glass window. She, at least, seemed concerned about her brother, another lost sheep.

Daire's smile faded, and he prayed for the young man. He prayed that Sam hadn't taken the heirloom. Daire didn't care about the legal implications of the figurine; he simply wanted it back. Needed it back. And her brother having stolen something would hurt Susan.

The idea of Susan being hurt by anyone twisted his heart, and he cut off that thought and focused on the sermon. He needed to hear all he could about redemption.

At last, they stood and sang the last hymn. Susan's voice rose pure and sweet, and a glowing peace settled over her face as she sang, "Jesus, lover of my soul, let me to Thy bosom fly, While the nearer waters roll. . ."

Listening to her instead of singing himself, Daire glanced

at her and experienced that wild-ride-through-the-rapids feeling in his middle. He hated to be rude, since he had accepted an invitation to dinner with the Morrises, but he needed to get away from Susan. Yet how could he expect to get the formula back if he did? People so careless with a living being wouldn't care much about an inanimate object they didn't even like.

The hymn ended. The pastor blessed the congregation and sent them on their way. Though he knew how the action would look to the assembly, he turned to Susan and offered her his arm out of the building. Behind him, he thought he heard Miss Deborah huff out a sigh of displeasure.

"I expect you're a bit worried about your brother," he said.

"I am." She nodded, sending a curl bobbing against her cheek and the flower petals on her hat fluttering. "He's never been gone this long. I'm terribly afraid—" She tilted up her head and looked directly into his eyes, hers nearly violet with emotion. "I'm terribly afraid you're right and he did take the goldfinch."

"But why would he do that?" Aware of everyone headed for the front door, Daire paused in the vestibule and edged into the aisle. "I spoke in haste, but with some thought, I can't imagine what a young man would want with such a trinket."

"To sell." Susan's fingers lay as light as thistledown on his arm, and she held herself farther away from him than even hoops necessitated.

"But neither of us did well trying to sell it. Why would he think he could?" He resisted the urge to cover her hand with his and draw her nearer—so they could talk more freely in the crowd, of course, nothing more.

Already they drew curious glances and a few knowing smiles or raised eyebrows. Miss Deborah started toward them. Mrs. Morris headed her off. Daire couldn't hear their conversation, but the looks cast in Susan's and his direction told him what the subject was.

"Sam might not know he can't sell it," Susan said. "He only knows I paid a lot of money for it, not that I couldn't sell it to anyone. And you sold it to me. Maybe if people around here knew about the Grassick Glassworks like Daddy does, they would find your goldfinch more valuable."

"Let's hope not." Daire led Susan out of the church in the wake of her substantial family.

At the door, the two brothers-in-law who'd gone hunting for Samuel waited without the youth. Their faces were grim.

"We didn't find him," one of the men announced. "He wasn't at home and he wasn't in the park."

"The lads in the park say they haven't seen him in a week," the other spouse added.

Susan's fingers tightened on Daire's arm, and a low moan emerged from her throat.

His heart twisted, and he touched her hand with his. "He can't have gotten very far since yesterday."

Yet even as he spoke, Daire reminded himself about just how much trouble a young man could get into in the city. Certain establishments flashed through his head, the bittersweet aroma, the raucous noise, the illusion of pleasure.

"Is he prone to disappearing?" he asked.

"Not like this." A stricken look contorted Susan's features. "I mean, he hates school and wants to go off on an adventure instead of to the university, but surely he wouldn't just pick up and run off."

"He might."

Daire pictured himself at sixteen, restless, no good at glassmaking, not interested in farming. . . .

"Shall we go back to your house and organize the search?" Daire suggested.

Now gathered around him, the Morrises looked at him as though he were some sort of miracle worker.

"That would be such a blessing," Mr. Morris said. "We're

not good at organization. But if you are, we welcome your aid."

He led the way down the church steps. The rest of the Morris family and others followed. Susan still held Daire's arm, and as they reached the main sidewalk, Deborah fell into step on his other side.

"You're very kind to help us, Mr. Grassick." Deborah spoke in a sweetly modulated tone. "I mean, we're really strangers to you, nothing more."

"He wants his goldfinch back." Susan's voice was sweeter than Deborah's, but her words sounded a little cynical, and he could do nothing to counter her claim.

"But that's what I mean." Deborah touched his arm. "If you hadn't bought it, he wouldn't have to bother with our ramshackle ways."

"If Miss Susan hadn't bought it, I might not have been able to find out who else had." Daire spoke the words to be polite, but once said, he realized they were true. "This way, I have a better idea where it could be."

"When we find Sam?" Susan's fingers flexed on his arm; then she released him.

Daire glanced at her, took in her set face, and wished he could assure her that her brother hadn't taken the object. Any number of people could have walked through their house without anyone knowing. But Sam Morris likely knew how much his sister had paid for the goldfinch, a lot of money to some, not enough to get a young man far unless. . .

But Sam wouldn't be in the sorts of places where Heath, Lucinda's father, lured the unwary and eager, Daire hoped. Those places, that scene, preyed on the young men who didn't have homes or families.

Minutes later, the entire Morris clan, minus one son, as well as several men and women from the church, gathered in the Morrises' back garden. Daire counted the men. Eighteen.

In moments, the eighteen men set out to various areas of the city. The ladies entered the house to prepare food and simply be near the Morris females as a comfort. Daire set out for the front gate alone. His destination was the harbor, a place much like the one he had sought as a young man, a youth like Samuel Morris, to find adventure. The one brother, Roger, had mentioned something about a clipper returned from China.

The front gate swung shut behind him with a clatter. Footfalls followed, the gate clanged again, and more heels clicked along the pavement. Daire paused, glanced back, and sighed.

"Mr. Grassick?" A gentle voice sounded behind him. A gentler hand touched his arm.

"Miss Morris?" He glanced down at Susan. "What is it?"

She tucked her hand into the crook of his elbow. "I'm coming with you."

"You can't." His response shot out with finality. "I'm—"

"Susan." Miss Deborah called from the front steps as she surged toward them on a froth of sky blue ruffles and lace. "You should be in the backyard helping with the children."

Susan's hand tightened on Daire's arm, but her face remained serene. "Opal and Daisy are here, along with a half dozen other ladies. They don't need me, but Mr. Grassick does." She cast him a pleading glance from beneath her gold-tipped lashes. "You don't know the city well."

"You didn't hear him giving everyone directions, did you?" Deborah reached the gate, laughing. "It sounded to me as though he knows it better than you." She tilted her head and gave him a coquettish smile. "But not better than I do. I do charitable work in some of the. . .less desirable areas, and we may need to look for Sam there if he's decided to get himself lost. I think I should go with you."

"I don't think either of you ladies should go with me." Daire touched Susan's hand on his arm. He intended to remove her fingers from his sleeve but found himself clasping her hand instead. "I'm going places that are inappropriate for a lady."

"I don't care." Susan tightened her hold on his arm. "I need to be useful. I won't be anything if I stay here." Her purplish blue eyes met and held his. Her chin set with determination. "No one will even miss me."

"Nor me." Deborah blinked rapidly several times as though clearing a speck from her eye, although a brightness to the blue suggested perhaps she was trying not to cry. "Gerrit didn't even come to help us look for Sam."

He wished he could disagree with the ladies on the notion that no one would miss them, but he feared both spoke the truth. The grandmother might. He spied her through the front window, nodding to something a befeathered matron was saying, but glancing out the window and nodding, as though she approved of her granddaughters vying for his attention.

"Miss Deborah, Miss Susan, please don't be foolish." Looking at their resolute faces, he felt his resolve become as wobbly as Deborah's chin. "These places I'm going if your brother isn't at the harbor could be dangerous."

"Then you shouldn't go alone, either." Deborah pushed through the gate and joined Daire and Susan on the sidewalk.

"But if you want to. . ." Susan released his arm and stepped back a foot. "If you don't let us go with you, I'll simply follow."

"I don't think your parents would like that." He made one last attempt to stop them.

Susan grimaced. "I wouldn't be so certain about that."

Remembering how Mrs. Morris had fawned over him—Mr. Morris, too, for that matter—Daire understood what she meant. Still, he glanced back toward the house in hopes of seeing someone he could employ to hold the ladies back. No one came into view, no one imploring them to return. In fact, the grandmother grinned and turned her back on the window.

He heaved a sigh and gave them a brisk nod. "All right, but stick close to my side and do exactly what I say."

seven

Susan frowned at her sister. Flirting a bit with Daire to make Gerrit jealous, Susan understood. It seemed to have worked, too, judging from the way he'd glowered at Daire in church. But Gerrit wasn't even there to see Deborah take Daire's other arm, nor hear her thank him profusely for allowing her to accompany him.

"I doubt you'll be thanking me in an hour or two." Daire's mouth set in a grim line. "Nor will your parents be pleased you two are with me."

"They'll thank both of us if we find our brother."

"All three of us," Deborah said. Then she launched into a line of prattle Susan doubted Daire would find interesting. "I think I've been in every part of this city. Momma and my sisters and I do a great deal of sewing for the less fortunate. My elder sisters, that is. Susan isn't good at sewing, so she stays home to see to things there."

Nicely put in her place.

Susan turned her face away from Daire and her sister and tried not to listen to Deborah go on and on about all her good works for orphans at home and now in India. Daire interspersed an occasional question, enough to keep Deborah chattering, and Susan said nothing. She trotted along at Daire's side, her heels clicking in rhythm with his and Deborah's, her skirt rustling. Few people moved about in the middle of a Sunday afternoon. Those who did smiled at the trio, the gentlemen lifting their hats.

Then the pavement grew less evenly distributed. Sidewalks turned into missing patches of brick, as though someone had hauled them away for building. The houses grew closer together until no more than a narrow passageway ran between buildings, and front doors opened directly onto the walkway. Men and women sat on the stoops, and dusty children played around them. Then the homes and people grew scarcer. Structures grew larger and taller. The aromas of spices and coffee, rope, and tar permeated the air, and the whistle of boat horns sounded through the towering building canyons.

"This isn't the harbor, is it?" Susan spoke up for the first time since leaving home.

Daire and Deborah paused to stare at her.

Her cheeks grew warmer than the mild spring day warranted. "I hear the boats and can smell the river, but it's never looked like this when we've gone anywhere by water."

"This is the warehouse area," Daire explained. "You probably took pleasure boats and left from the passenger side."

"Yes, of course." Susan ducked her head and wished she'd kept her mouth shut.

"As much as I've enjoyed the walk," Deborah said, sounding a bit winded, "I don't know why you'd think Sam would be down here."

"Miss Susan said he wants adventure." Daire smiled down at her. "I tried to go aboard a merchantman when I was about his age. But if you need a rest, I'm certain we can find someplace to let you ladies sit while I ask around."

"You can't leave us alone here." Deborah glanced at a towering warehouse. "Some of the people who loiter here are unsavory at best."

"No, this is no place for a lady." Daire's jaw hardened. "But you two insisted you come with me or follow me, and coming with me seemed the safest course for the two of you."

"I was hoping—" Susan looked at her sister and snapped her teeth together.

In no way would she admit in front of Deborah that she hoped their parents would be proud of her if she helped to find Sam and bring him home. And she couldn't admit to Daire she preferred to find Sam if he was guilty of stealing the goldfinch bottle.

"Sam's always been a good boy." Deborah filled in the silence left by Susan's refusal to talk further. "I think once he sees the two of us, if we do find him, he'll realize running off is foolish. But—oh dear."

Susan followed Deborah's gaze to where an old woman slept in the doorway of one of the storage facilities.

"Doesn't she have a home?" Susan whispered.

"Probably not." Daire sighed. "There are too many people living like that since the financial panic last year."

"That's so sad." Susan glanced at the grimy buildings and litter in the gutters, and her throat tightened. "I never go anywhere to see things like this."

"Your family protects you." Daire touched the back of her hand. "Should I take you home? Things might get uglier than this in another block."

"Not like that poor old lady," Deborah said. "The harbor area is just full of sailors, but they might make some vulgar remarks. If you ignore them, though, they'll go away."

"How do you know this?" Susan stared at her elder sister.

Deborah shrugged. "I come down here once a week."

"You—" Susan thought her eyes would bug from her head.

Daire looked bemused, too. "Why does a gently bred lady come down here once a week?" he asked.

"I help make food for men and women who don't have work." Deborah ducked her head so the brim of her hat hid her face. "Mostly I serve food, since I'm not a very good cook."

"You—" It was all Susan could get out for a moment. After a long breath, she managed, "But I thought you were at the church sewing or trying to get donations for the orphans."

"Not on Mondays." Deborah kept her face averted.

Susan's eyes stung with tears. "And you never asked me to join you? You know—"

The clatter of boot heels on pavement and raucous voices interrupted her.

"Perhaps we should have this discussion elsewhere." Daire started forward, away from the noisy men. "I'd rather not be here with two lovely ladies when that lot comes around the corner."

Susan fell into step with him again, and Deborah did the same. The rowdy men emerged from an alleyway a hundred yards behind them. Even from that distance, their ribald remarks swept toward Susan's ears. Those ears grew hot, and the heat spread to her cheeks.

"Just ignore them," Deborah advised. "They'll lose interest. They won't do anything in daylight. It's nighttime that is dangerous."

"How do you know all this, and who do you come here with?" Susan blurted out the questions. "Momma and the others wouldn't come down here."

"No, but Gerrit does." Deborah's voice fell so quiet, Susan nearly missed the words beneath the blast of a steamboat whistle. When they sank in, she understood Deborah's reluctance to talk about her excursions to this sad part of town—her heart hurt over Gerrit's reluctance to propose, or lack of interest in proposing. That he hadn't come along to help search for Sam was troubling. Sam looked up to Gerrit.

"We'll just have to be the ones to find Sam," Susan declared aloud. "Regardless of what these sailors shout to us."

"It can be pretty rude," Daire cautioned. "Your parents aren't going to like me bringing you here." He glanced at Deborah. "I admit I'm surprised they let you come every week."

"They'll let me go anywhere with Gerrit Vandervoort." Deborah grimaced. "They never ask where we're going, they trust him so much."

Susan blinked. She thought her parents ignored only her whereabouts, but they seemed to pay little attention to Deborah, too, and, obviously, Sam.

She wanted to stop and ask Deborah if she thought they didn't care or if they trusted their children to behave themselves. But the unruly men gained ground behind them, and she sensed Daire wished to enter the greater crowd near the harbor, so she picked up her pace and said nothing, her heart partly more burdened and partly lighter. She liked knowing that her sister sometimes felt neglected, too, but felt burdened that frivolity filled her days, especially since she'd inherited Great-aunt Susan Morris's fortune.

Pensive, she scarcely noticed her surroundings until the sweet notes of a hymn drifted through the shouts of boatmen and cacophony of the steam engines.

"It's a church." She stopped and gazed at the whitewashed building perched amid the warehouses and wharves like a pearl amid boulders. "Why is there a church down here?"

"It's a mission to the sailors," Deborah said.

"You know a great deal about the work going on down here." Daire gazed at Deborah with admiration.

Susan felt sick. All she could tell him about was the best place to buy hats or how to get raspberry jam out of a carpet.

"I didn't want to be a useless spinster," Deborah said, returning Daire's look of approbation, "so I started asking around about how I could serve. Gerrit Vandervoort brought me down here with some other people from the church a few years ago, and I've come ever since."

"I thought he was courting you with the intent to marry you," Susan said. "At least you've led the rest of the family to believe it."

Such an expression of pain crossed Deborah's face, Susan immediately regretted her words.

"I'm sorry." She wished Daire weren't between them so she could take her sister's hand. "That was mean of me, but we really did think. . ."

"So did I." Deborah coughed. "Let's go into the mission. I'd like to rest while Mr. Grassick looks for Sam."

"But he doesn't know what he looks like."

"He has a sketch." Deborah released Daire's arm and crossed to Susan's side. "Come along. They'll enjoy hearing you sing."

Susan remained where she stood, though she saw two sailors ogling her and Deborah. The mouths of the men moved, but the noise around them blocked their words from her hearing, for which she was grateful. "But I need to find him. If I do—"

No, she couldn't admit to Deborah that she wanted to be the one to bring Sam home so her family would notice her, would admire her for something. In light of the new revelations about Deborah's work in the poor part of town, it made her look selfish and mean.

"Miss Deborah is right," Daire said. "I may need to go inside places a lady can't go into if I don't find him along the wharves."

"We'll be inside." Deborah tugged on Susan's arm.

Still reluctant, Susan paused outside the church that was no larger than the first floor of their house and perhaps smaller. A box had been nailed to the side of the structure and filled with soil and flowers. She reached out one hand and stroked a scarlet tulip petal. "I wonder if this came from Holland."

"Possibly." Daire averted his gaze from her, as though he didn't like the sight of her.

No wonder. Old people slept in doorways, and her sister served food to the needy once a week, while she bought fripperies from an inheritance given to her to catch a husband. All she'd caught so far was a glass bauble important to no one but the man beside her, who seemed interested in her sister, if he didn't simply want to find his family heirloom and get away from all the Morrises.

"Let's go inside," Deborah urged.

Susan nodded and followed her sister through the doorway

so narrow they each had to turn sideways to accommodate the breadth of their hoops. A few people glanced at them, men and women alike, and smiled. Susan returned the friendly greetings and slipped between two backless benches at the rear of the room. The singing continued. After a moment, Susan joined in the familiar words, letting her voice soar with the others.

She didn't realize she sang alone until the chorus ended and a ragged older lady, who smelled like boiled cabbage, turned and clasped Susan's hands.

&

From inside his coat, Daire removed a sketch Gran Morris had given him. Sam apparently resembled his father, as did Susan. How to find one youth among the throng of men and boys Daire didn't know, but he began to show the sketch around and ask if anyone had seen such a young man. The answers varied in politeness. The result was the same—no one had seen him. Finding a stack of unattended boxes, Daire climbed atop them and scanned the crowd from his height advantage. He caught no glimpse of maple syrup–colored hair, though a hat would obscure that if the lad wore one.

What Daire did see made his gut tighten. Besides the dozens of mostly men, who seemed not to care that today was a Sunday, he noted two establishments with which he had grown too familiar over the past months, businesses owned and operated by Lucinda's father. Establishments set up to lure in and swindle the unwary young man seeking adventure or easy profit.

Samuel Morris wanted adventure, according to his sister, and might wish to turn an easy profit to fund that adventure. If he had taken the goldfinch and discovered, as Daire had, that it wasn't worth a great deal of money, he might find his way—or be lured into—one of Leonard Heath's establishments.

Knowing he had to look, Daire darted across the thoroughfare and into a building he'd sworn he would never enter again.

Even on a Sunday, men of all ages sat playing their games of chance while discussing business that was as much a game of chance as the dice and cards. Those vices hadn't lured him, but the prospect of making lots of money quickly had. He'd thought he would go home rich, making up for his lack of talent in farming or glassmaking with his independence.

He shuddered, took too deep a breath of the smoky air, and scanned the room for a familiar face.

"Grassick," someone called. "You're looking prosperous. Ready for another venture?"

The room erupted in laughter. Daire had been a great dupe for these men, who took from the unsuspecting to invest in land in the West or railroad stock that might be worth something if the tracks went across the plains someday. Daire had fallen for the scheme. The only game that hadn't taken him in was the prospect of work in the West. He didn't want to be that far from home.

Seeing these men, knowing they operated inside the law just enough to keep them from getting prosecuted while taking people's hard-earned money or inheritances, he wished he weren't as far from home as he was. He wanted the strength of his family's love.

You need the strength of the Lord, he heard his father saying.

In his head, Daire knew Father was right, but at that moment, he thought of how disappointed his family would be if he fell back into his old ways. How ruined they'd be if he failed to find the goldfinch and the formula.

"I'm looking for someone," he said as though the man hadn't spoken. "A young man with eyes the color of wisteria—"

Laughter burst out in a roar.

"Turned poet now that you're penniless?" another man taunted.

"Only until the railroad moves west," someone else pointed out. "Then he'll be rich."

Daire glanced at the cards in front of the man and expected

his investments had gone into a game of chance and not any railroad stock.

Daire smiled. "Perhaps. But it's the most distinguished feature about him."

"He wouldn't come in here without money." Heath strolled from a back room, a gold watch chain gleaming across his vest. "How are you, lad? Lucinda misses you."

Daire tried not to picture her beautiful face, hear her sweet voice. He should think of Susan or, perhaps better yet, Deborah. She possessed a giving spirit along with her beautiful face.

"Give Miss Heath my regards." Daire injected polite coolness into his tone. "I'm looking for the brother of some acquaintances. He may have been carrying my goldfinch bottle, trying to sell it."

"Haven't seen him or it." Heath's dark eyes gleamed. "I'd have bought it off him if he had. Discovered it's more valuable than I realized."

"Indeed?" Hairs rose across the back of Daire's neck and along his arms beneath the sleeves of his white linen shirt. "How's that?"

Heath shrugged. "One of a kind from the glassworks Queen Victoria uses."

"You already knew that."

Had he somehow discovered the formula had been hidden inside the goldfinch? No, not possible.

"I didn't realize that made it valuable." Heath laughed, while the other men fell silent. "Lucinda said I never should have let it get away. Or you, for that matter. You know you're welcome back at any time. I think she pines for you."

Temptation flashed through him. Lucinda was always orderly, purposeful, determined. He had felt secure in her presence.

He shook off the image of her in his head. He didn't need to feel secure in a person. Security came from the Lord, his family had reminded him. He wanted to be with them for more of that reminding.

He gave Heath a polite smile. "Give her my regards, but I've had enough of life up here. I prefer to be with my family."

"Doing what?" Heath started to laugh.

Others joined him.

"If this young man comes here"—Daire held up the sketch—"please send word to the Main Street Hotel."

A few people nodded as though they'd heard him. Doubting them, knowing too much of their lack of generosity and kindness, Daire spun on his heel and exited.

Despite the sourness of garbage from a nearby alley, the air outside smelled as fresh as the Morrises' garden compared to the reek of cigar smoke, macassar oil, and fear inside the building he'd just left. He considered calling on another establishment where Heath lured young men in with false promises, but a glance down the street told Daire the windows were dark, the curtains drawn.

He heaved a sigh of relief and headed to the church. As he approached the doorway, one voice stood out against the background of steam whistles and rough talk. A clear soprano sang with a warmth and sincerity that brought a lump into his throat. After his visit to Heath's business and thoughts of calling on Lucinda, however fleeting, he felt unclean, not worthy to step into the presence of such beauty of spirit. Yet feeling as though the singer had attached a length of Mr. Goodyear's vulcanized rubber to his belt to draw him in, Daire charged to the church.

He paused in the doorway. The church's coolness and peacefulness closed around him like loving arms. With a glance about, he realized that the singer was Susan. She caught his eye, faltered, and stopped.

Everyone faced Daire.

"I apologize for interrupting." He twisted his hat in his

hands. "I came to collect the ladies."

"We've enjoyed having them for our hymn singing." A burly man with a peg leg thumped down the aisle toward Daire. "The young lady has been a blessing to us all."

"Oh no, I—I just like to sing." Susan's face turned as pink as her hat.

Deborah gave her younger sister a bemused look. "And I never knew you could sing like *that*. How have we missed that. . . ? Well, never you mind. Maybe we can come back someday."

"Please do." The man, who seemed to be the spokesman for the congregation, though he didn't wear the typical suit of a pastor, held out his hand to Daire. "Jeb Macy. I lead this mission now that my sailing days are over. We have a singin' every Sunday and Wednesday. Come back and bring as many as you like."

"I'll do that if I'm still around." Daire shook the man's calloused hand.

He hoped he wasn't around that long. By Wednesday, he would be in the arms of his family again with the formula in the glassworks safe. Yet part of him felt a twinge of regret that he wouldn't hear Susan singing again, nor the rest of these people, whose faces glowed with a joy he had never understood, even with all his worldly goods.

As he led Susan and Deborah out of the mission, a chorus of thank-yous and invitations to return followed them. He wished he'd found this church in the city instead of Heath's comrades. If he had, he would have returned home and all would be well.

"Why don't you sing like that around us?" Deborah demanded of Susan once they reached the sidewalk. "You know the rest of us can scarcely tell one note from another."

"Momma told me not to sing loudly whenever I go to church," Susan admitted. "She said I am showing off and—" She turned abruptly toward Daire. "Any news?"

"Not from the men I asked." He took her hand and tucked it into the crook of his elbow. Deborah took his other arm without invitation. "So we should look for him at the harbor."

"Why?" Susan's fingers flexed on his arm. "Surely he isn't trying to run away, is he?"

"I don't think he would consider it running away," Daire said.

"He is always fascinated with boats," Deborah added. "Gerrit and I caught him down here one day. But that was about a year ago, and we scared him off, we thought."

"Young men can get adventurous." Daire gazed at the smokestacks protruding into the blue sky, many puffing out clouds of steam and soot like the glassworks' chimneys. "We can only hope he hasn't gone aboard somewhere."

They headed toward Elizabeth Street and the harbor. Daire gave a brief account of his inquiries.

"So he hasn't tried to sell the goldfinch to men who deal in stolen goods," he concluded.

"I see." Susan started to remove her hand from his arm.

"Please don't be angry." He stopped, pulled free of Deborah's grasp, and caught hold of Susan's fingers. He held them. "You need to understand the possibility."

"I know." She blinked rapidly and hard. "I just can't bear the idea of my brother taking something that isn't his and running off. I mean, it's obviously not valuable or you would have been able to sell it to these men."

"I could have, but I wouldn't." He resumed walking. "They're not nice people."

"How do you know?" Deborah and Susan asked together.

"To my shame, I did some business with them."

Deborah gasped. "You dealt in stolen goods?" Horror filled her voice, rising above the blast of a steam whistle.

"No." He wouldn't tell them the rest.

"Then how—" Susan stopped. "I suppose it's none of my concern if you help me find my brother."

"Someone will find him." Daire cast a quick smile in her direction. "Tell me about the church. Did you enjoy waiting there?"

"I did." Her tone turned reverent. "Those people looked. . . Well, they're not prosperous. But their joy glowed from them. It's almost as though. . ." She paused in the middle of the sidewalk and gazed up at him. "It's almost as though they believe every word they sing and pray, as though they really believe God is with them."

"You don't?" Daire's stomach clenched with the sorrow that coursed through him.

She shook her head. "God doesn't have time for me. I'm too unimportant."

"Susan—I mean, Miss Morris, God has as much time for you as He does everyone else who wants it."

"Then why. . . ?" She started walking again. "Let's look this last place for my brother."

"All right, but we should talk more—"

Daire stopped himself. No, they should not talk more. He needed a young lady certain in her faith. Never again would he care about a female who went through the motion of worship without feeling it in her heart.

Silence stretched between them. Deborah made no more move to take his arm, though she kept pace with him and her sister. Beneath Deborah's bonnet, her face looked still, pensive. A furrow creased Susan's smooth brow.

As they drew closer to the harbor, the noise of the steam engines and whistles made speech difficult anyway. With relief, Daire noticed several ladies amid the crowd around the docks, embarking or disembarking passengers from pleasure cruises on the river. Susan and Deborah didn't stand out, and although a few men cast admiring glances Susan's way, no one said anything inappropriate. Like him, she turned her head and looked at everyone. He could only guess at Samuel Morris's appearance. Most of the men were older, though, weathered sailors and stevedores, or middle-aged sightseers, so Daire hoped Samuel's youth would make him stand out. He saw no one he could even guess was the young man.

Beside him, Susan gripped his arm and tipped up the brim of her hat. "I wish I were taller. Maybe if I stood on—" Before he knew what she was about, she released his arm, darted forward, and clambered onto a crate.

"Susan, that doesn't look very stur—"A crack like gunfire penetrated the noise around them as the lid of the crate split.

Daire lunged forward to catch her, but she leaped to safety and kept going, plunging into the crowd, her hoops pushing people aside more effectively than strong elbow thrusts. Daire followed and caught her cry.

"Sam. Samuel Morris, stop right there." She then flung herself onto a gangly youth with rumpled clothes and maple-colored hair.

"Aw, Sue, what are you doing here?" The boy held her off at arm's length. "This isn't a place for a lady alone."

"I'm not alone." Susan grasped Sam's shoulders and shook him. "I'm with you, and I'm with Daire Grassick and Deborah. Now what are you doing scaring us all, taking off like this? If I were Daddy, I'd—oh, you make me so angry. Did you take the goldfinch?"

eight

Sam stared at Susan as though she'd lost her reason. "Why would I take that piece of yellow glass?"

"Because it's valuable." Susan glanced at Daire, realizing she'd just admitted her brother could be a thief. "It's a unique piece of glass made by the Grassick Glassworks."

"But you couldn't get anything for it." Sam's upper lip dusted with a pale line of fuzz, curled in the slightest of sneers. "And he had to sell it to you to get any money for it."

"Mr. Morris," Daire said in his rich timbre, "you should show your sister more respect."

"Respect Susan?" Sam laughed.

Susan flinched as though he'd struck her. "Really, Mr. Grassick, I'm just his sister."

"You're a lady and deserve to be spoken to with courtesy." Daire frowned at Sam. "Now if you please, answer your sister with a civil tongue."

"Susan's not a lady." Sam kicked at a crumpled piece of paper lying on the wharf. "She doesn't do anything that—"

"She's spent the afternoon in the heat helping me look for you." Daire's voice, still low, cut through Sam's protest.

Susan looked at Daire, feeling as though she had been set aglow like a lantern in a dark room. No one ever championed her, except for Paul upon occasion. But Daire had done so with Gran yesterday and now Sam today.

If she wasn't careful, she could fall in love with this man. Deborah's arched eyebrows told Susan her older sister saw the danger signs, too.

Sam ducked his head and ground the toe of his boot into the wharf. "She didn't need to. I should've been gone by now, but the paddle wheel broke on the *Mary Sue*."

"You really were running away?" Susan forgot Daire slipping into her heart and his goldfinch and Sam's disrespect of her. "Sam, why?"

"I don't want to be a banker." Sam gestured to the line of vessels from the tiny pleasure crafts to the enormous seafaring ships, and to the river leading to New York City on the other side, then the sea beyond Long Island. "I want to see the world. India. China." His voice took on an awed tone. "Rio de Janeiro. I want to do something. . .important, not be just another one of the Morrises no one can keep track of."

"Oh Sam." Susan blinked back tears. "I wish I didn't understand how you feel."

"But running away isn't the answer." Daire rested a hand on Sam's shoulder, making him look like the boy he still was. "I know. I did it more than once. No good ever came from it."

"Did you go to sea?" Sam's face lit.

"Just a riverboat the first time." Daire turned Sam toward the street. "I'll tell you about it while we walk back to your house."

Sam balked. "I don't want to go home. The captain of the *Mary Sue* hired me on. My gear's already aboard."

"You're too young," Deborah protested.

"When is she due to leave?" Daire asked.

Susan shot him a disapproving glance. Surely he didn't intend to give in to her brother's insistence that he remain at the docks.

"Tomorrow now." Sam made a face. "Can't get the wheel fixed on a Sunday, so we missed the tide last night and this morning and tonight. Probably won't be until tomorrow night now."

"Then you've got time to go home and persuade your father to give you his permission." Still gripping Sam's shoulder with one hand, and with Susan and Deborah falling into step behind him, Daire headed away from the harbor.

"Wouldn't you rather go with your father's blessing?" His voice drifted back to Susan's ears.

"I won't get it." Sam sounded like a sullen ten-year-old rather than the grown and independent man he wanted to be. "He'll go write a poem about sailing out to sea."

"You shouldn't talk about Daddy like that." Susan bristled. "His poems are beautiful."

"They're useless, just like Momma's and Deborah's sewing and—"

"That's enough, laddy." Daire's tone turned steely. "Families are to be honored and cherished, not scorned."

"But mine—"

"Was terribly worried when they discovered you were missing," Daire said, cutting off Sam's protest.

"Yeah, and how long was I missing before they figured it out?" Sam gave a stone in the road a vicious kick.

"It was too long, Sam." Susan felt as though her bodice and hoop skirt had grown too big for her. She hastened her steps so she could walk beside her brother. "Will you please forgive me? I've been so concerned about myself, I didn't give you a thought."

"What do you have to be concerned about?" Sam demanded. "You got all that money from Great-aunt Susan. You can pay your way to anywhere you want to go."

"I can't pay for—" Susan stopped and glanced sideways at Daire.

He'd already learned too much about her family yesterday and today. She wasn't ready to share her heart, her disappointments and frustrations, any more than she had already revealed to him.

Not to think of Deborah overhearing revelations of her younger sister's heart. Deborah was oddly quiet, her face set, but not like someone who was angry—more like someone deep in difficult thought.

"I was sixteen the first time I ran off." Daire spoke into

the silence broken only by the crunch of their footfalls on the walk and the voices of passersby. "I hopped aboard a boat going up the Delaware River. My father was in the middle of harvest and didn't miss me either. He thought I was working where I was supposed to be because he trusted me to do my work. So my grandfather came after me. He left an important customer to find me and bring me home." He fell silent.

When he said no more for an entire block, Sam asked, "What kind of trouble did you get for that?"

Susan was glad he'd asked and she didn't have to.

"None." Daire's face grew sad. "We got home to find my father had fallen asleep over his supper he was so weary from doing his work and mine, too. And the next month, Grandfather showed me the books to the glassworks and how much money the company lost because of my escapade."

"That must have stung," Susan murmured.

"Not enough," Daire said. "I left them again."

"No one loses sleep or money by me leaving." Sam snapped a low-hanging branch off a tree and began to whip it through the air with a hoarse whistle as they walked. "They won't have to feed me, so it'll save money."

"They'll lose your school fees," Deborah spoke at last. "You'll never get into university."

"I don't want to go to university." Sam smacked the branch against a fence, snapping the limb in two. He tossed the pieces onto the sidewalk.

Daire stopped. He said nothing, just stood motionless staring at the litter.

Susan opened her mouth to tell Sam to pick up the broken branch. Before she formed the words, her brother glanced at Daire then retrieved the sticks with a muttered apology.

"Leaving your family will hurt them," Daire said. "At least ask for permission."

"I'll never get it." Sam sounded more sad than sullen.

Susan wanted to cheer him. "You know Momma and

Daddy don't say no to you, Sam."

"But if they do—"

Two men stepped from a side street, and Sam halted his speech and body.

"Daddy," Susan called. "We have him."

Their father spun on his heel and strode toward them. A smile lit his face. "You're all right, son."

"Yes sir." Sam took the hand his father stretched out to him and shook it. "I signed on to the *Mary Sue*. She's a merchantman headed for Madagascar. I don't want to give up my berth on her."

"Well, now, we'll have to talk about that." Father and son strolled toward home.

The other man, a member of the church, nodded at Susan and Deborah, shook Daire's hand, and followed.

A lump swelled into Susan's throat. She grasped the picket of a neighbor's fence, heedless of how the rough wood could snag her glove, and blinked hard against the moisture in her eyes.

"Miss Morris?" Daire moved to stand in front of her. "Are you all right?"

"Yes, I'm just. . .embarrassed." A shudder ran through her. "You've spent your afternoon hunting down my brother, and no one even thanks you. And we aren't any closer to finding your goldfinch."

"Your father was happy to have his son home safe." Daire touched a fingertip to her cheek, and she realized a tear had rolled there.

"He's here at last," Deborah murmured, her gaze fixed on the house and a handful of men milling about the front garden.

Gerrit leaned against a pillar of the front porch, one hand shielding his eyes, as though he gazed into the distance for an incoming ship.

Or maybe just his lady.

"It's far more important to bring home a lost lamb than a piece of glass."

"Well yes, but—" Susan snapped her teeth together to keep from bursting out that her father hadn't noticed her back home, either, or that she'd even been gone; it sounded selfish, as though she should be more important than her brother. She didn't want that. She just wanted to be *as* important. For once, she wanted them to notice her above all the others.

"Let's go home," Daire said. "You must be tired and hungry."

"I am." Susan took a handkerchief from her reticule and dabbed at her eyes. "And let me thank you if no one else does."

"Seeing him safe is thanks enough." Daire offered her his arm then held out his other arm for Deborah.

She declined it and ducked behind Susan and Daire. Thus, the three of them completed the last two blocks to home. Most of the people remained from earlier. Children ran about the yard, playing a game of tag. Inside the house, women had set out food on the dining room table. Sam sat with several other men, explaining about the *Mary Sue* in between and around bites of ham and salad.

Gerrit was nowhere to be seen, and Deborah had also vanished.

Good. Perhaps they would mend their fences and Gerrit would speak up at last.

The notion that Deborah would be engaged at last saddened Susan. She'd wanted it so she would be the last daughter at home, but she'd glimpsed a different side of Deborah today and wondered if perhaps she was ignoring her sisters as much as she believed they ignored her.

Hoping to find Momma, Daisy, and Opal in the kitchen, Susan turned to Daire. "Go join the men. I'll bring you a plate."

"Why don't you sit down and let me bring you a plate."

Daire smiled at her. "You look tired."

She instantly wished for a mirror to see how bad she must appear for him to say her fatigue showed.

"Thank you," she began instead of rushing off to find a looking glass. "I think—"

"Mr. Grassick."

Momma and Daisy descended upon them—or more accurately, Daire. Their faces beamed. Plates of food filled their hands.

"Thank you for bringing Sam back to us." Daisy shot her brother an indulgent glance. "He's such a wanderer I think they should just let him go off somewhere."

"But he's too young," Momma protested. "Don't you think, Mr. Grassick?"

"It depends on the captain," Daire said. "If he's a good, Christian man, the experience could be good."

"Just what I said to my husband not two minutes ago." Daisy gestured across the room. "I told him to save you a chair. Do sit down."

"I think Susan needs the seat more," Daire said.

Susan gazed up at him. Her middle felt like melted caramel. Her heart. . . She feared she'd just lost that.

Momma and Daisy glanced at Susan as though they'd just noticed her, which they probably had.

"You look tired," Momma said. "What have you been doing?"

"I was looking for Sam with Deborah and Mr. Grassick."

"You were?" Momma and Daisy said together.

They narrowed their eyes in twin speculative gazes and glanced at Daire then back to Susan.

"Clear a space at the table for Susan, too," Momma said.

"I was going to get Mr. Grassick some food." Susan gestured toward the buffet. "He gave up his day for us."

"Nonsense." Daisy's smile glowed with all its beauty. "You were out, too. I'll bring you a plate, as well."

Before Susan knew how to respond, Momma and Daisy ushered her to the table and made her sit beside Daire. Within moments, plates of food and glasses of lemonade rested on the cloth before them. Momma and Daisy fawned over Daire all the while they served, as they had earlier at church. Some of their effusiveness spilled over onto Susan, mainly because Daire sat turned in his chair to look at her and included her in every remark. In those minutes, Susan received more attention from female members of her family than she had since bringing home the goldfinch.

Because of Daire.

She cast him a sidelong glance. He was a remarkably attractive man and so very kind. Best of all, her family liked him. If she managed to attract him, her family would notice her because she'd be with him.

As soon as the notion struck her, she dismissed it. It seemed far too mercenary to set her cap for a man because her family liked him. On the other hand, she remembered the way his touch, the sound of his voice, simply being near him made her feel warm and pretty and. . .needed.

Only until they found the goldfinch. Or until he gave up seeking the bauble.

She fixed her attention on her plate. She mustn't even let herself for a moment consider a match with Daire Grassick. A man like him would want a far prettier girl and one with a family that didn't lose one of its children for a whole day. Daire came from the sort of family that married heiresses.

And she was an heiress.

She squirmed on her chair, her appetite gone. She couldn't let herself be interested in Daire for more than a passing acquaintance. She thought she was starting to have strong feelings for him, but maybe they came from the attention she received when she was in his company and not from the man himself. Only time would show her the truth, and she didn't have time with him.

Daire seemed to have his attention fixed on the dialogue between the other men and Sam. They discussed the good and bad aspects of allowing her brother to head off to Madagascar—wherever that was—with an unknown sea captain.

"You could get to know him," Daire suggested during a lull, while Deborah circled the table with a pitcher of lemonade. "If the *Mary Sue* isn't leaving port until tomorrow night's tide, you could invite him here for a talk or go down there to the docks, Mr. Morris."

"Well, um, yes, I suppose I could." Daddy's face turned ruddy. "Not, um, much good with strangers, but for my son. . ." He cast a frantic glance to Sam.

Poor Daddy. He was shy. Susan wondered why she'd never noticed that before. She thought he didn't talk to any of them because he didn't care. But she couldn't think that with the way he had panicked over Sam's absence earlier and now looked at the eldest son as though he were truly a precious gift.

If he just looked at her like that once, she would never feel unimportant.

"I'll take you to him." Sam's face lit as though he had a lamp inside his head. "He has a good reputation. I asked around before I approached him."

"That shows maturity," Daire murmured to Susan.

"All right." Daddy took out a kerchief and mopped his brow. "Tomorrow. No, no, it'll have to be tonight. Tomorrow is a workday. Hmm. It'll be difficult to find the man after dark, and it's getting on to that. I don't know, Sam."

"Father." The glow on Sam's face died. "I'll show you where the boat is."

"I'll go with you, Mr. Morris." Daire set down his fork. "If you've finished eating, we can leave right now and be at the docks before the sun sets."

"Why would you do that?" Susan couldn't stop herself from asking. "We're strangers to you."

"We'll go, too," William and Marcus said.

Susan kept looking at Daire, waiting for an answer.

He glanced from Sam to Susan. "I understand what he wants. If the captain is a good man, it could be the best thing for your brother. He'll either find what he wants and have a career started, or he'll keep running off until he finds what he wants and too likely end up in bad company."

"Have you found what you want from running off?" Susan thought her tone was a bit sharp but didn't understand why.

"I have found one thing"—Daire spoke with an even cadence, though the corners of his eyes and mouth tightened— "that nothing is more important to me than my family. I just wish—" He pushed back his chair and rose. "Mr. Morris?"

All the men rose. Susan followed. She knew she would never be allowed to go to the harbor with the men, but she walked with them to the entryway, clinging to the fringe of the group in the hope someone would notice her. Someone like Daire Grassick. She wanted to say good-bye to him. All too likely, he wouldn't return. They'd lost his goldfinch bottle. *She'd* lost his goldfinch bottle. He had no need to return. And now Sam was likely to leave her. She never paid much attention to her brother, but she didn't like seeing him leave, heading off for the other side of the world for months or years.

As though he felt her gazing at him, or perhaps he was simply polite, Daire made his way to her side. "May I call on you tomorrow?"

"Ye–yes." Susan's heart began to gallop so hard she thought her lace fichu should start fluttering as though in a high wind. "I didn't think—there's no need. . ."

"Perhaps the two of us can think up another place to look for the goldfinch," Daire said.

"I don't know—yes, maybe we can." Susan felt breathless. "Tomorrow. The goldfinch has to be somewhere around here. Maybe Gran has seen it after all, or—"

"I did see your goldfinch yesterday." Sam turned around, blocking the doorway and everyone's exit. "I'm sorry I didn't tell you earlier." He looked down and ground his toe into the floorboards, scuffing them. "I didn't like being dragged home like a recalcitrant schoolboy, so I didn't say anything."

"What are you talking about, son?" Daddy asked.

"That glass goldfinch." Sam looked up at Daire. "I honestly don't know where it is, sir, but I saw a man with it. He was heading toward those tenements on the other side of Market Street."

nine

Daire didn't think Samuel Morris should exchange his family for the discomfort of shipboard life and a voyage to the other side of the world. He was too young to be on his own. Yet he wasn't impulsive as Daire had been. Samuel thought out his plan and executed it. If not for a broken paddle wheel, the lad would be well into the Atlantic and beyond his family's reach to draw him back. If he didn't go with their blessing, he would succeed in making his escape the next time.

Why he was aiding these people, who were near strangers, in managing their recalcitrant son, Daire didn't know. But there he was, striding along beside the other men in the family and discussing the merits of travel, something none of them had done much of beyond crossing the Hudson River to go into New York City or traveling south to Philadelphia. All the while, Daire waited for the opportunity to talk to Sam alone and ask him more details about seeing someone with the goldfinch bottle. From the sound of it, finding the bauble again sounded hopeless unless Sam knew the identity of the man or could describe a unique characteristic that would help in identifying him. Daire suspected that was a vain hope and the goldfinch was forever lost.

Its precious secret gone forever or, worse, waiting to be found by strangers.

He cringed at the notion of unknown hands retrieving the formula and either throwing it away as useless or recognizing its value and selling it to—whom?

Heath had said he would buy the goldfinch now, that he hadn't known its value when Daire might have, in desperation, sold it to him. Was it possible that Heath knew the formula lay inside the goldfinch? No, not possible. He couldn't have learned that in just a few days.

Except that Leonard Heath could have learned something. He knew far too much about far too many people for Daire to doubt the man's ability to gather information on the Grassicks. He had done business with them, after all. He'd infiltrated the family, using his daughter as a lure.

Which meant Daire would have to rejoin the Heath social circle to learn if his notion held any merit.

His gut tensed at the idea. He would try to get information from Sam.

He maneuvered himself so that he fell into step beside the youth. "Why do you want to run away from people who love you?"

The others grew quiet, including Sam. He ducked his head as though the brick sidewalk at his feet required all his focus.

"I suppose if your father gives you permission to leave, it's not running away," Daire amended.

His father had given him permission to leave the last time. He'd spoken his disapproval of Lucinda and her crowd, but he had given Daire part of his inheritance to invest, to make a go of life on his own.

"But the world can be cruel to a young man without proper guidance," Daire continued. "It's none of my concern, but I speak from experience."

"We won't let him go if the captain isn't a good man," Mr. Morris said. "I'd rather Sam finishes school and goes to university."

"I don't like school." Sam raised his head and brushed his hair out of his eyes. "I'm no good at mathematics or reading."

"Your work was fine this past term." Mr. Morris set a hand on his son's shoulder as they neared the harbor. "I was pleased."

"Then tell Susan." Sam's face grew flushed. "She helped me through."

"Susan?" The chorus of male voices rang out against the walls of warehouses and shipping offices, as though no one recognized the name.

Daire glanced around, reading astonishment in faces lit by the setting sun. Not one of them believed Susan had aided in the attainment of Sam's schoolwork to a degree that he had earned good reports.

"She's excellent at arithmetic," Sam said. "I always put the numbers backwards and end up with the wrong answer if I try it on my own. And she helped me figure out my sums and get my reading straight."

And Susan thought she didn't pay enough attention to her family or think they noticed her? Sam did. No wonder she wanted to find him.

"Once I started to read better," the youth said, his face lighting, "I looked through the books in Father's study and found some about faraway places. I wrote a report for school on India, and the teacher read it to the whole class. And, well—" He shrugged. "I want to see more than words about a place. If I could write things after I see the place, it might make people here think about the people there and maybe that would help Momma and the girls with this mission and. . ." His voice trailed off, his cheeks turning more scarlet than the sunset.

"I never knew, son." Mr. Morris stopped and brushed a hand across his brow. "I just read about those faraway lands and dream in verse, but I never thought to go see them."

"Then let me, please, sir." Sam fairly bounced from foot to foot as the group recommenced their trek to the harbor.

"We'll see what the captain's like," Mr. Morris said.

"Or perhaps find a better one?" Daire suggested.

Unlike him, Sam held a purpose in his desire to wander, and Daire wanted to see the youth attain his goal, if his soul and body would be safe.

If Daire had known a reason for his wanderings other than

the vague notion of proving himself as good at something as were his brothers and sister, he would not have sought after easy wealth and gotten himself mixed up with the wrong sort of people and damaged his relationship with his family and God.

If only he possessed a purpose for his life now, then—what?

No no, he must find the goldfinch, take it home, and do what his family wanted of him, whether that was acting as a mere clerk in the glassworks or plowing fields alongside his father, regardless of how both activities made him restless and longing for something more for his life, some sort of. . . purpose.

His lips twisted in an ironic smile. He would have no work with the Grassick glasshouses, and possibly the farm, if he didn't find the formula inside the goldfinch before someone else did.

Someone like Leonard Heath.

Regardless of whether the gesture appeared rude and intrusive, Daire clasped Sam's shoulder and drew him away from the other men. "Tell me more about the man you saw with the goldfinch. How do you know it was my—the piece your sister purchased from me?"

"Couldn't mistake it." Sam frowned. "I thought maybe she managed to sell it after all, though the man didn't look like he had enough money to buy something like that."

"What did he look like?" Daire pressed.

"Well, he was kind of tall." Sam frowned and rubbed the bridge of his nose. "Kind of your height. And his hair was about your color. Dark. And he wasn't quite so broad in the shoulders." He shrugged. "Can't think of anything else."

"Can you tell me where he went?" Daire kept his tone even, trying not to sound too eager and encourage Sam to forget details out of nervousness or make something up to get Daire to stop asking questions. "You said something about a tenement."

"Yeah. They're like a rabbit warren there near the harbor.

Lots of sailors' families live in them. Lots of Irish who came here from the famine."

A rabbit warren. Lots of families living in tight quarters.

Daire knew the place, knew of its cramped, dark apartments with rooms like railroad cars shared by a dozen family members and facilities in the yard the entire building used. Finding one man who was roughly his height and coloring amid that crowd was impossible even if he didn't get assaulted and robbed the minute he stepped into the throng of immigrants trying to survive on too little money and even less hope.

Those were the young men Heath tried to lure into his schemes, promising them jobs out west. Hope sprang into the faces of those men—hope that they could support their families and find a better life for them away from the city. They disappeared west, but no one ever heard from them again. Daire had found out why. Heath gave them jobs mining, digging wells on land Heath owned so he could sell it for more money—backbreaking labor for which they never saw a cent because. . . Heath had provided Daire with a dozen excuses, none of which Daire accepted. The men needed clothes, so Heath provided them—for a fee. They needed transportation and food and shelter. Heath provided them—for a fee.

No one heard from the men, because most took off on their own or died or simply could not afford the cost of postage back to family members who too often couldn't read.

Daire's hands balled into fists at the memories of how his involvement with Heath had helped fund such adventures. Except Heath and his cronies were the only ones getting rich from land deals and mines.

Heath again, a man who could easily pay one of those men in the tenements to steal the goldfinch.

Jaw tight, Daire addressed Sam again. "Can you think of anything else?"

"No. Sorry, sir." Sam looked sincere, though his gaze quickly traveled from Daire to the harbor and a stocky steamboat, whose name blazed across her bow in silver gilt lettering: *Mary Sue*. Closer inspection showed a clean deck and smokestack. The sailors working around the deck spoke to the visitors with respect, and no foul language passed between them. If the captain proved to be responsible for this behavior, which was likely, Daire decided he would take advantage of his seeming influence with Mr. Morris and encourage him to let Sam go to sea. A lad with a purpose should be encouraged.

❧

Catching sight of Deborah at last, Susan balanced a stack of dirty plates on her hip and charged out the back door. She didn't care that her sister and Gerrit Vandervoort stood in what appeared to be serious conversation, judging from their set faces and tight lips. Susan couldn't wait any longer to talk to Deborah about her work with the mission and possibly the people in the tenements, where someone carrying Daire's goldfinch bottle had disappeared.

"Are you going to wash those in the well?" Deborah asked.

"What? Oh." Susan set the plates on the grass. "Deborah, do you know people in the tenements?"

"I wouldn't say I know them—"

"Miss Susan," Gerrit said, breaking into Deborah's hesitation, "will you ask about that later? Your sister and I were having a talk about—"

"We all know Bridget," Deborah interrupted in turn. "She lives there with her sister and her sons. I believe they all work—or try to work—on the docks, when there's work, that is."

"Bridget." Susan felt a little ill. "Deb, you don't think Bridget would take the goldfinch, do you?"

"It's useless," Gerrit said. "Why would she take it?"

"Because it's pretty," Deborah snapped, "and she probably

doesn't have many pretty things."

"But she's never taken anything from us before," Susan protested.

"We don't have frivolous ornaments lying about, either." Deborah half turned her back on Gerrit and faced Susan fully. "And it was tucked behind the pictures because none of us wanted it. She might not have considered it stealing any more than it's stealing if she takes leftover food home with her."

"But it's wrong to take things anyway." Susan twisted her fingers together. "We told her she could take the food. Taking the goldfinch is. . .different."

"Then ask her in the morning," Gerrit suggested, sounding bored.

"I will." Susan picked up the plates and marched back to the house.

But in the morning, Bridget didn't arrive for work. Everyone scurried about so much trying to get Sam off to his ship and the younger boys off to school, despite their protests that they wanted to watch Sam sail, Susan didn't take time to wonder about the maid's whereabouts until Daire arrived at the front door.

"There's your young man." Gran chuckled and dropped a sketch onto the floor.

Susan picked it up while Deborah answered Daire's knock. The drawing showed a young man with wild dark hair puzzling over a young lady and an adult human–sized goldfinch, as though trying to choose between the two.

"You are so droll, Gran." Susan kissed her grandmother's cheek. "But please hide this one away." She tucked it at the bottom of the stack. "He's not in the least interested in me. He just wants his glass ornament."

"And he doesn't need you to find it, now that he knows you don't have it."

"But I have information for him."

It wasn't much, but it was a gossamer thread of hope.

"He doesn't know that." Gran grinned and bent over her sketch again.

Susan turned toward the front hall, where Deborah laughed with a flirtatious note, and Daire's deep voice rumbled in return. "He could be here for Deborah."

"Deborah will marry Gerrit when she's done making him suffer."

Susan glanced back at Gran. She'd started outlining a drawing with a man holding up his hands in supplication.

"Is that Gerrit?" she asked.

Gran laughed. "I give him another week."

"Or less." Susan smiled and headed into the hall.

"Good afternoon, Miss Susan." Daire bowed. "Miss Morris tells me that your brother got off to his ship safely."

"Yes, thank you. I've never seen him so happy."

"Knowing one's purpose in life can make a body happy." Daire gazed past Susan, as though something important hung on the wall behind her. "I've seen it in my family."

"But not you?" Susan dared to ask the question.

"Not as much as I'd like." Daire shimmied his shoulders as though shaking off rain and turned his brilliant smile on Deborah. "You will help me search today, won't you? You know something of the tenements, you said."

"I do, but Susan has more information than I do right now." Deborah gave Susan a little nudge on the arm. "Go ahead without me. Today is my day for the soup kitchen with Gerrit."

"But—" Susan didn't want to go without her elder sister. "I don't know where Bridget lives."

"If you can't find her," Deborah said, "I'll come with you tomorrow."

"Deb—"

"Time's wasting." With another trill of laughter and a wave of her hand, Deborah swept out of the entry hall and up the stairs.

"I don't know if it's proper for me to go with you alone," Susan murmured, her cheeks growing warm.

"We'll always be in the daylight." Daire held out his hand. "And your family approves of me." His lips twisted into a mocking smile at this last.

Susan squirmed. "They approve of you being a Grassick."

"It's approval nonetheless." His smile turned genuine. "And I'd like to hear about what this Bridget has to do with our search."

"She's our maid," Susan began.

By the time she finished her tale, she wore her bonnet and a light shawl and was strolling down the pavement with her hand tucked into the crook of Daire's elbow.

"But I don't know where she lives," she concluded.

"You have a full name," Daire said. "That will help."

"But I—" Susan halted, her face burning with shame. "I don't know her last name. That is, I'm not certain of it. O'Malley? Mulligan. I—I never asked her."

She wished the maid stood before her so she could ask her forgiveness, ask her last name, ask about her family and native country and hopes.

Daire started walking again. "We'll find her. I found you, after all, and with little trouble, and I didn't even have so much as your Christian name."

"My Christian name." Susan mused over the familiar reference to a first name. "I wonder why it's called that, when so many of us don't deserve it."

"Don't you consider yourself a Christian?" A muscle bunched at the corner of Daire's strong jaw.

Susan gnawed her lower lip. "Well, I mostly help with the children at church, but I don't attend services much. And my Bible is dusty from disuse. And now—" She stopped.

Just because she was gaining a great deal of attention from Daire Grassick didn't mean she should unburden herself to him. A man who was little more than a stranger didn't want to hear about how she felt neglected and yet, apparently, did little herself to pay attention to others.

"I don't think God has much interest in me," she finished.

"He does, Susan." Daire covered her hand with his, sending a thrill all the way through her. "I thought He didn't care about me, either, but I realized how wrong I was when I went home and my family welcomed me with unconditional love and acceptance. God used their kindness to remind me that He always loves us, regardless of how we behave, and I have behaved far more badly than you ever could have."

"I'm completely self-centered." She made herself look up at him. He was gazing down at her, so she met his gaze full on. The intensity of his green eyes made her stomach clench and her mouth go dry. She wanted to blink, break the connection, but she felt rooted to the pavement. A passerby bumped her hoop, sending it swaying, and still she couldn't move.

"Who are you?" She asked possibly the stupidest question in the world and tried to cover up for her silliness. "I mean, I know your name is Daire Grassick and your family makes glass, but I don't know anything about you, and yet—" No, she would not say she felt as though she knew as much as she needed to, to know to experience a yearning in her heart far stronger than any wish she felt to have her family proud of her for something.

"I come from Salem County, where my grandmother's family has lived for over a hundred years." Daire started walking again as he talked, his words emerging slowly, as though he chose each one with care. "My grandfather came from Scotland nearly fifty years ago to work in the glassworks. We also have a large farm. But I'm not much good at farming or glassmaking, and I didn't want to just take orders while the others worked. So I came up here to make my fortune."

"But you didn't?" She posed the query but knew the answer. He hadn't. He'd sold her the goldfinch.

"Why Hudson City and not New York?" she asked in addition.

He remained silent for so long she thought he wasn't going to answer. Amid the crowd of Monday morning shoppers and clerks running errands, she wasn't certain she would have heard him. They walked through the heart of the city, past her great-aunt's bank, past her father's bank, past the pawnshop where she'd seen Daire for the first time.

And started dreaming of him as more than a person in a chance meeting like a shopkeeper?

Oh yes, she dared admit that now. The man, as much as the goldfinch bottle, had caught her attention, with his good looks and air of bewilderment. She wanted to help him, make him smile, encourage him to smile at her. And when he had, she yearned for attention from him, as she had never wanted it from her family. And all he wanted from her was help finding his goldfinch, a silly, frivolous piece of glass.

"Leonard Heath encouraged me to come here." Daire spoke so abruptly Susan jumped. "He did business with my family, and his daughter. . . But that's all behind me now unless Heath wants the goldfinch."

"Why would he want it?" Susan asked. "Surely, he knows it's not valuable."

"It's more valuable than I realized." He guided her around a bit of broken pavement.

They had entered the less prosperous part of the city, where the shops grew dingier and the houses narrower and more crowded.

"How could it increase in value?"

Had she not made a foolish acquisition after all?

"I'd rather not say any more than—" Daire paused and stared down the street toward the tenements. "My family will be ruined financially if I don't find it."

"Goodness me." Susan blinked up at him. "Surely you exaggerate."

"Perhaps a little." Daire shrugged. "We'll still have the farm, but we could lose the glassworks."

"Oh no." Susan wished to run down the street, calling Bridget's name aloud.

Instead, she paced along beside Daire until they stood across the narrow thoroughfare from the first row of tenements. Courtyards nestled in the shadows of the three-story buildings, courtyards mostly full of women, children, and old men. Some washed clothes at the single pump each building offered. Others cooked over open fires, sending the greasy tang of cheap sausages and smoke into the humid air. Others simply lazed about, their faces devoid of joy or—

"They look so hopeless," Susan murmured, her eyes stinging with tears.

"They are, mostly. That's why men like Heath can take advantage of them. He promises hope, where he delivers none."

"Does God care about them, too?"

"Most definitely."

"Then why are they so unhappy?"

"Unless we seek Him, we all are without the Lord in our lives, regardless of how much money we have."

The words struck home. Susan opened her mouth to ask him more questions, but a swarm of children surged toward them, hands outstretched. "Sweets?" they demanded.

"No, but I have—"

When she reached for her purse, Daire stayed her hand. "Not coin. Too often bigger children or even adults take it from them for gaming or drink."

"But they look hungry," Susan whispered.

"They probably are." Daire smiled at the youngsters. "I'll buy you some meat pies if you can tell me where to find Bridget."

"Bridget who?" the children demanded. "Bridget O'Malley? Bridget O'Halleran? Bridget McConnell?"

Susan felt her own hope slipping away with each name the children mentioned. The muscle tightening in the corner of Daire's jaw warned her he felt the same.

"All of them," Daire finally said.

They got directions. With a gaggle of youngsters following them, they sought out and found ten Bridgets. None were the Morrises' maid. None claimed to know who she was. The morning slipped into afternoon with no progress. Susan's feet felt as though her shoes were made for one of the little girls trailing in her wake, and her stomach growled loud enough to mimic a steam engine. Daire proved relentless, though, climbing steep, narrow steps that smelled of cabbage and other things Susan didn't want to consider, or ducking down alleyways that sent fear crawling up her spine for fear they would meet more than another Bridget at the end.

At last, he paused to buy a dozen meat pies from a street vendor, handed them out to the children, who stuffed the pastries into their mouths, and divided the last one between Susan and himself.

"You look tired." He traced a fingertip along her cheekbone. "I should take you home. Perhaps your Bridget has come to work by now."

"Maybe." Susan thought her face must reflect the hope-lessness of the people in the courtyard. "But even if she hasn't come to work—especially if she hasn't come to work—I should go home and make dinner and see if the boys need help with their schoolwork. And Gran is all alone unless Momma came home for lunch. I must stop neglecting my family. Maybe then—" She turned her face away.

"Yes, let's stop for today. It's getting too late to remain here." Holding her hand instead of letting her take his arm, Daire led her out of the tenements and back to the more prosperous part of the city.

Once she trod on pavement with shops and houses she recognized, Susan expected she would feel less downcast, less. . .

hopeless. But the feeling remained, a deep sorrow eating away at her heart like rot on a piece of fruit. There she was, with more money than she knew how to spend, unable to spend it on anyone beyond herself in any meaningful quantities, and she was so very unhappy. She had a fine home, if somewhat neglected, and a family, also neglected, and her heart ached. The most attractive man she'd ever met held her hand, and she wanted to crawl into a private place and weep.

To her relief, Daire didn't try to talk either, though he kept a firm, warm grip on her hand, as though he needed the contact. As though he welcomed the contact.

As though he liked the contact.

But no, not her. He wouldn't be attracted to her that way. He came from an old family, a famous family. He would want a girl who came from the same sort of people, not an heiress with selfish intent.

Nor one who couldn't say specifically that she was a Christian.

They arrived home to find Gran munching bread and jam in the kitchen.

"I've never seen you without your sketching, ma'am," Daire greeted her. "I'm pleased to see you up and about."

"Need to be if you're going to drag my granddaughter all over who knows where." Despite the sharpness of her words, Gran grinned, showing her still good teeth. "Of course, if you enjoy her company, I won't complain."

"I do enjoy her company, ma'am." Daire drew a chair out from the table. "Do sit down, Miss Susan. I see the icebox. Will it have something cold to drink inside?"

"I made lemonade this morning." Susan didn't sit. "But you sit. I'll serve."

"Sit down, girl," Gran ordered. "You look like you're about to fall down."

"I'm all right," Susan declared.

Then she burst into tears.

ten

Daire swung away from the icebox and stared from Susan to Gran then back to Susan. His sister, Maggie, never cried. He had no idea what to do with a weeping female.

"She needs comfort," Gran said in an exaggerated whisper. "Or maybe just a nap."

"Then I'll leave." As much as he wished to, Daire couldn't bolt with Susan so distraught.

"I'm all right," she insisted again, drawing a handkerchief from a pocket in her gown. "Those poor people just made me so sad, and I can't help them. I'm rich, but I don't have control of my money and can't help them."

"Where did you take her today?" Gran asked.

"To look for your maid." Daire's heart felt like lead in his chest—guilt, regret, and understanding of Susan's feelings. "We saw many people who aren't doing well in life."

"And I'm so selfish, I just want attention from everyone." Susan buried her face in her hands. "But the bankers won't give me control of my money."

"Then you'll have to get married," Gran pronounced. "Your aunt wanted you to use that money to catch a husband." She glanced at Daire from the corner of one still sharp eye. "A nice Christian man."

"I don't deserve a nice Christian man." From between her fingers, Susan's face shone as red as strawberries, but not unattractively so.

She cried rather prettily. Rather appealingly. Daire's arm twitched with the impulse to wrap it around her shoulders, draw her close so she could weep on his shoulder.

Before he realized what he was doing, he did just that. She

felt so tiny against him, except for the ridiculously wide skirt women found necessary to parade about in to fulfill fashion's demands. He imagined protecting her always, offering her the shelter of his name, the abundant gift of his family's love. Together they could—what?

His lack of a purpose in life kept him from doing something truly foolish like kissing her in front of her grandmother, which would have been tantamount to a proposal. He didn't know Susan well enough for that.

Yet he'd run off to the city, away from his family, after a far more brief acquaintance with Lucinda.

And that was all the more reason to take himself off, as far away from Susan Morris as he could. But not while she grasped his shoulders like one of his own grandmother's kittens clinging to a limb by only their front paws. As the kittens trusted him to lift them to safety, Susan seemed to expect him to lift her spirits from despair.

"If you can't give them money," he suggested tentatively, "perhaps you can work alongside your sister, serve them food, take care of their children so they can get some rest or even do a little work."

"Do you think I could?" Her voice sounded as tiny as one of those kittens, too.

"You could," Gran broke in, "if we didn't need you at home."

A shudder ran through Susan, and she drew away from Daire. "I'm not needed here. I do so little for any of you. I even left you alone all day."

"You spoil me, child." Gran reached out a hand with fingertips bearing testimony to the many colors of her pastels. "As you see, I'm not as helpless as you let me behave. And the boys—"

The cries of children outside echoed Gran's words about brothers.

"They're home, and I look a fright." Without so much as

another glance at Daire, Susan fled from the kitchen, her bonnet dangling down her back.

"If you're only interested in having her help you find that piece of bric-a-brac," Gran said, her jowls quivering beneath a set chin, "then I suggest you stay away. We take advantage of her desire to please us so much, she's going to fall in love with the first man who pays her attention—as you are."

"Yes, ma'am." Daire smoothed his damp neck cloth. "I'm in no position to consider courting a lady right now. Though if I were. . ."

He couldn't finish that sentence. He didn't know if he could court Susan even if he did know what he was supposed to be doing with his life.

The kitchen door burst open, saving him from having to speak of Susan any further. Two youths charged into the house, faces shining, books tucked under one arm. Immediately they dropped the books onto the floor.

"Where's Susan?" the younger one cried. "I'm starving."

"Mind your manners," Gran ordered. "We have company."

The boys halted and nodded to Daire. "Good afternoon, Mr. Grassick. Are you here calling on Susan?"

"No, I'm just leaving." Daire shook the boys' hands and bowed to Gran. "Thank you for your words of wisdom, ma'am. I have taken them to heart."

And, for no logical reason, his heart hurt at the notion of not seeing Susan again.

And with the realization that, with no success at finding the Morrises' maid, he had no choice but to visit Leonard Heath—and Lucinda.

&

If she could crawl under her bed and hide, Susan would do so. But the raucous entry of the boys reminded her she was going to pay more attention to her family, and that meant feeding Paul and Roger, helping Gran back to the parlor, perhaps even making dinner, such as it would be with her poor cooking skills. She could only hope that Daire had gone home to his real home, far from Hudson City, so she wouldn't even accidentally encounter him. After her mortifying display in the kitchen, she doubted she could face him without dissolving into a puddle of humiliation.

She was of no use to him now that she couldn't find Bridget or any other clue to the whereabouts of his goldfinch. He wouldn't be back. She needed to stop dreaming about him caring for her and find a way to make her life valuable to others so God would want her. Somewhere in her mind, she was sure that if God and she shared a relationship, she didn't need anyone else. But He wouldn't have any more use for her than anyone else unless she did something special like her mother and sisters did.

Momma and the eldest girls didn't want her to work with them, but maybe Daire was right and Deborah would let her hand out food on Mondays. Surely one had an easier time finding hope in life if one had a full stomach.

The notion of full stomachs reminded her again of her brothers. She splashed cold water on her face from the basin in her room then tidied her hair and descended to the kitchen in time to stop Paul and Roger from devouring all the bread in the house.

"Go to the bakery and buy more," she told them. "We won't have anything for supper if you don't, since Bridget didn't come to work today."

"Did she steal that glass thing?" Paul asked. "I mean, it disappears, and she stops coming to work."

"It's possible." Susan thought of all the tired women in the tenements. "Or maybe someone needed her more than we do. Now, run along. I'll help you with your schoolwork when you get back."

"We want to play ball," Roger protested.

"You'll have enough light to play ball after you do your schoolwork. Where's Gran?"

"She got herself back to the parlor." Paul scooped up a crumb with his moistened fingertip and popped it into his mouth. "Can we buy sugar buns?"

"One apiece if they have any left, but you can't eat them on the way home. Not until after supper." Susan shooed the boys out of the house then set about cleaning up dishes and trying to work out what the family would eat for supper.

All the while she worked, she thought of how to ask Deborah if she could go with her. Maybe they could even go more often. In the end, for all her practiced speech, she simply asked outright.

"I'd love for you to join us," Deborah responded without hesitation. "I didn't think you'd like it, or I would have asked you to come along."

"Why did you think I wouldn't like it?" Susan asked.

"Because you seem to like to stay here at home. Even after you inherited Great-aunt Morris's money, you didn't even try to spend any of it for months."

"And look what silliness I created when I did spend it." Susan picked up the hem of her skirt to examine a tear in the bottom flounce. "If I hadn't bought that goldfinch—"

"You wouldn't have met Daire Grassick." Deborah's eyes glinted with gentle teasing.

Susan feared her eyes sparkled with tears. "There's nothing in that. I can't help him find his bauble, and he's gone off to hunt for it on his own. Or perhaps reacquaint himself with the lady who had lured him to Hudson City instead of new York or Philadelphia."

Deborah clasped Susan's hands in hers. "I'm so sorry if that's true. But he'll come back if he cares."

"He's only interested in his goldfinch. And I need to be interested in some sort of good works like what you're doing."

"It's little enough." Deborah sighed. "We fill their bellies and hope we show some of God's love through this small act."

"Can we do more?" Susan wanted to stamp her foot like a

child. "If only I could spend Great-aunt's money, I could—oh, I don't know. But it's wasted on me. I don't need a husband to do good for you all and for those poor people and to show God I want to be a Christian."

"Being a Christian takes more than just doing good, Susie, or even going to church. You need to give your heart to Him and trust in Him and serve Him as He directs you."

Susan crossed her arms over her middle. "Does God lead us in a direction even if I don't—I mean, haven't—given my heart to Him?"

"Yes, it's possible." Deborah looked thoughtful. "Everything that happens in life has a purpose God uses."

A tingle of excitement raced through Susan at the notion that maybe God did notice her, had been leading her in a direction after all.

"If I hadn't bought that goldfinch from Daire and lost it, I wouldn't have realized that we have so many needy people right here on our doorstep," she added. "Momma and Opal and Daisy, and you, too, are always worrying about children in India, which is important, but what about the children in the tenements? They're so sad, so lost, so. . .hopeless."

She gazed up at her elder sister. "Is feeding them enough to give them hope?"

"No, not for long enough. They need to know that they have a future to look forward to."

"How can we give them that future?" Susan began to pace about the kitchen, where Deborah and she had been cobbling together a supper of bread, cold meats, and salad. "Isn't there land out west? I heard about how a man promises people land but never delivers on it. But what if they had real land, learned how to farm—or maybe they already know how—and were given a way to get out there and make claims in, where would that be?"

"Iowa, Illinois, Kansas. . ." Deborah sounded thoughtful. "But that would take a great deal of money, Susie."

"Which I have and can't use for anything but catching a husband." Susan banged the teakettle onto the stove. "And what husband would want to spend my money like that? He'll want to spend it on himself."

"Not the right husband." Deborah chuckled. "You need a man with his own means and a sense of responsibility. A man like Daire Grassick."

"Daire Grassick will never be back. I'm not good enough for a man like him."

"What are you talking about?" Deborah slipped up behind Susan and rested her hands on her sister's shoulders. "Why do you think you're not good enough for Daire Grassick?"

"I want attention for myself and I'm not good at much but singing."

"I would have said that a day ago, but now I realize that you have a kind and generous heart and we've all been so good at saving the world around us that we've forgotten our little sister needs some guidance, too."

"Guidance toward what?" Susan faced her sister. "I've tried to join Momma and you and Opal and Daisy with the mission work, but only so you'd notice me, not because I cared about poor children in India."

"And you feel differently about working with the kitchen at the tenements?" Deborah's eyes turned deep blue with her seriousness. "Or do you want to glorify Susan?"

"I want to help. I know now there's so much suffering there. I want to give them hope."

"We can fill their bellies for a day, Susie," Deborah said, her voice a little rough. "But true hope comes only from God. Do you understand that?"

"I. . .don't know."

Daire had said something similar. Maybe if she hadn't given the wrong response to him, he would be coming back.

"I hear the boys coming." Deborah cocked her head to one side. "And Father will be home soon. But after supper, I'll read some scripture with you. The Bible says things so much better than I can."

The boys flung themselves through the back door right then, bearing bread loaves, sugar buns, and telltale dustings of the latter confections around their mouths. Susan didn't scold them, though she knew she should. She was too preoccupied with thoughts of hope beyond the material, not to mention the practical matters of helping the boys with their sums and reading, then finishing preparations for the meager supper.

"We must find out what has happened to Bridget," Momma said as she dissected a slice of tomato. "Your father needs a hot meal after a day at the bank. If Sam were here, I'd send him to her flat, but maybe you can go, Susan, if Roger and Paul accompany you."

Susan stared at her mother. "You know where Bridget lives?"

"Of course I do." Momma looked indignant that Susan even needed to ask.

"And do you know her last name?" Susan pressed.

"Yes." Momma arched one perfect golden brow. "It's McCorkle."

Susan jabbed her fork into a sliver of hard-boiled egg. "Then I'm happy to go."

ॐ

"I wondered how long you would stay away." Lucinda swept into the parlor in a red silk gown over wide hoops, her raven hair scooped atop her head like a crown, her dark eyes brilliant with triumph. "Papa said he saw you wandering about looking prosperous again. Did your daddy fill the coffers with more money to invest in our little schemes?"

"Good evening to you, too, Miss Heath." Daire gave Lucinda a formal bow, ignoring her taunting query. "You are as lovely as ever. Are you going out tonight? I don't wish to keep you from your friends."

"Oh, la, they're not important compared to you." Her voice

purred. She tossed her head, sending curls dancing over her bare shoulders and wafting the scent of attar of roses into the crowded parlor.

Not so long ago, that voice, the gesture with the bouncing ringlets, and the aroma of roses stirred Daire. Now he thought of Susan's lilting voice, speaking truth as she saw it, light and pure, of her maple-syrup curls tumbling over a modest fichu with artless grace, and her light fragrance more reminiscent of sun-warmed grass than bottle perfumes. Her mere smile or the brush of her fingers thrilled him more than all of Lucinda's flirtatious gestures.

Tamping down images of a young lady he mustn't care about for far different reasons than he had applied to stifle feelings for Lucinda, Daire injected a chill into his voice. "I doubt your father feels that way, depending on the company."

"But no, dearest Daire." Lucinda laid her hand on his arm and squeezed. "Papa would love for me to renew our engagement."

"Yes, the Grassick fortunes would make a nice addition to the Heaths'." Daire removed her hand from his arm and stepped out of range of her reach. "When will he be home?"

"You mean to tell me you came to call on him?" Lucinda's full red lips pouted. "And here I thought I was the lure. I'm crushed."

"For your father, not for any interest you have in me."

"Daire, you're so cruel." A tightening around her eyes made Daire wonder if she spoke a fraction of truth in her latter words.

"You were. . .at first." Daire softened his tone. "But I need a Christian wife willing to live in the country near my family, and if you're honest with both yourself and me, you'll admit that isn't what you want."

"Well no." Lucinda sighed. "I often wished it were." She fingered one of her pomaded curls. "I think I was a little in love with you. But church and the country are so boring compared to parties here in the city."

"Then why did you set your cap for me?" Daire hadn't meant to bring up this much of the past, yet the words sprang to his lips, and he couldn't help but let them emerge.

"Papa promised me a wedding trip to Europe if I could get you to the altar." Lucinda laughed. "So you see, your value is high."

Daire felt a little ill.

"What about when the honeymoon was over?" he asked.

"No one in my set spends much time with her spouse." Lucinda settled herself onto a chair, her skirts billowing around her like a pile of discarded petals. "But since you don't like Papa's promises of how he can make you rich one day, and you don't want to marry me, why did you come back?"

"To find something that belongs to me." Daire didn't sit. He remained on the far side of the room. "My goldfinch bottle is missing, and I want to know if you or your father have anything to do with that."

"Your goldfinch bottle? Daire, Daire, Daire, you are so unnaturally attached to that hunk of glass. Forget about it and find a nice girl to marry instead."

Jaw set, Daire remained silent, meeting and holding Lucinda's gaze. Her words told him she knew something about the goldfinch. Otherwise, she wouldn't be telling him to forget about it.

She broke the eye contact first and let out a titter. "Why would you think we would know anything about it? Last I knew, you were trying to pawn—" She covered her mouth with her hand. Above the white fingers, her eyes clouded.

"How do you know I wanted to pawn it?" Daire questioned in a low, intense voice.

Lucinda shook her head.

"Your father was looking for it, wasn't he?" Daire pressed.

Lucinda blinked. She didn't confirm his claim. Nor did she deny it.

"Why?" Daire persisted. "I know he isn't trying to get it for you. You were so careless when I showed it to you that you nearly dropped it on the floor."

"No, I have no interest in a silly little glass bird," Lucinda burst out. "But if I'd dropped it, getting the formula would have been so much easier."

eleven

Susan wore an old gown without hoops for her foray into the tenements with her brothers. She'd spent the day cleaning the house and studying a cookery book to come up with a meal that was more substantial than bread and cold meat and salad. The stew she left simmering on the stove smelled savory, though she didn't like the looks of the layer of grease on the top. Bridget's stews never bore the slimy stuff when she served it. Maybe she could find a way to scoop the nasty substance away before they ate it.

Or maybe she could persuade Bridget to come back to work. If the maid did return, Susan vowed to learn how to cook. Even if being a true Christian and real hope came from God, as the Bible said, she thought He might appreciate a lady who possessed useful skills, too, even if that lady would always have enough money to live on, while paying someone to cook for her.

And if all You want is my heart, God, she prayed silently as she marched along between the two boys, *then show me what that means.*

Deborah explained how all Susan needed to do was ask, but Susan had given up asking for things when her mother and sisters said no to her coming along to help them.

Yet Deborah hadn't said no the day before, had she? On the contrary, they had acted like close sisters ever since.

"Can it be that simple?" she murmured.

Paul and Roger glanced at her.

"What did you say?" Paul asked.

"I was talking to God," she told them.

"I do that, too," Paul said. "I ask Him to take care of Sam

and keep him safe."

"I asked God to find me boys who can hit a ball as well as I can, but He hasn't answered it," Roger piped up.

Susan laughed. "Roger, do you think God is some kind of rich uncle who hands out toys at Christmas?"

"It was worth a try." Roger grinned. "Paul plays all right, but he's still too short."

"You miss when I pitch to you." Paul swung his arm for demonstration.

"Only sometimes."

"Only most of the time."

"Not once yesterday."

"Boys." Susan headed off an argument. "I want you to stay with me until we get back home, just like Daddy said you must. If we get separated, we might never find one another again."

"We'll all just go home then." Paul flipped onto his hands and began to walk.

Passersby stopped to stare.

"Paul," Susan tried to snap between chuckles, "you're not in the circus."

"But I don't have any schoolwork tonight." He righted himself. "How much farther do we have to go?"

"Another two blocks, I think—where's Roger?"

Sometime during Paul's antics with a handstand, Roger had rounded a corner ahead of them and encountered a throng of boys his age and older, batting a dilapidated ball and racing from point to point in the interminable game Roger loved to play.

"He caught it!" Paul cried. "Did you see that, Susan? Roger caught their ball from a block away."

"I saw it." Susan raised her voice. "Roger, get back here."

He either did not hear her or chose to ignore her. Cheered on by the group of youths, her middle brother threw the ball. For whatever reason he did that, it must have been good, for half of the boys cheered and the other half booed.

"Go get him back, Paul," Susan directed.

"All right." Paul plunged into the melee—and disappeared.

Susan cried out in protest but could do nothing to retrieve either brother unless she, too, ran into the crowd surrounding and participating in the game.

Daire wouldn't have abandoned her on the pavement.

Yet Daire had abandoned her, not sent a single word of regret or appreciation for her help. Not that she blamed him. She had lost his precious family piece. Even if it was hers, she should have taken better care of something that bore more sentimental than monetary value.

Without his chivalrous attentions, she must extricate Paul and Roger by herself.

Clutching her shawl across her front like a shield, she edged her way into the first circle of youths. They elbowed her back with rude remarks, the kindest of which was, "No girls here."

"But my brothers—"

A cheer and chorus of whistles drowned her out.

"Paul, Roger," she tried to shout above the tumult.

The shoving boys grew more insistent.

"Go bake bread or something," a young man a foot taller than her suggested. "Leave them to their fun."

"But I need them to help me find—" She stopped.

The youth had turned his back on her, blocking her view of the playing field—the street.

Extracting her brothers looked impossible, and she still needed to find Bridget. Maybe if she did, the maid would help get the boys away from the game. She always could manage them better than anyone else.

Glad she had left the hoops off today, Susan slipped away from the rowdy boys, glanced about for someone she could ask for directions, and headed toward a slip of a girl with a baby in her arms. "Will you tell me how to get to Mulberry Street?"

"Thataway." The young woman pointed with her chin to a narrow alley appearing dim in the shadow of the tall, narrow flats. "Why you want to know?"

"I'm looking for Bridget McCorkle." Despite the warmth of the day, Susan shivered at the notion of going into that tangle of passages alone.

But she would go, for Daire's sake. For Bridget's sake. Maybe even for her own sake—she didn't know.

"Please." She licked her dry lips. "I need to find Bridget. Not to cause her any trouble," she added with haste.

The girl shrugged. "Turn left, then right, then right again—" She thrust out her hand. "I'll take you."

For a fee. Susan understood the gesture and dug in her purse for a nickel.

The coin disappeared down the girl's bodice, and without a word, she turned and stalked toward the first street. Susan followed, ignoring some catcalls from a group of lounging men. In the girl's footsteps, around refuse and cooking fires, corners and crooked passages too narrow to be called streets, Susan trod with care. She feared the girl led her astray, they turned so many corners, but kept up the walk with dogged pursuit until, at last, the young woman pointed to a white-washed door.

"There she lives."

Before Susan could thank her or pay her another nickel, the girl and her too-silent infant disappeared back into the warren.

"Wait," Susan called.

What would she do if Bridget wasn't there? She could never find her way out again. "Please, come back. I'll give you another—"

The whitewashed door opened. For a heartbeat, Bridget, solid and white-faced, stood in the frame. Then she spun on her heel and vanished into the flat.

"Bridget, stop." Susan raced in after her.

One dark room led to another. All lay empty, silent save for the patter of fleeing footsteps, sparse of furnishings and spotlessly clean.

"Bridget." Susan slammed into a door painted the same whitewash as the flat's walls.

She staggered back, holding her bruised nose. Her head spun. Stars danced before her eyes. And the silence grew intense inside, not much louder beyond the walls.

Still holding the bridge of her nose with one hand, Susan opened the door. A courtyard lay beyond. Many women worked there washing clothes, tending to children, cooking on braziers. None of them was Bridget.

੨੬

Daire experienced a lightness of spirit he hadn't known since leaving home in pursuit of wealth and Lucinda Heath. At last, he'd shed his heart and soul of any lingering interest in her. Yes, she was beautiful. Yes, she could be charming. No, she was nothing like what he wanted in a wife.

He wasn't certain what that was and refused to contemplate it at present. Each time he did, while walking back to his hotel from the Heaths', while eating his breakfast, while planning his next step in finding the goldfinch, he saw Susan's pretty face.

Susan Morris was most definitely not right for him either. Yes, she was pretty. Yes, she was sweet-natured and open and honest in a refreshing manner after the Heaths' set of friends. But her family needed her. She didn't think they did, but that they depended on her presence at home appeared obvious to Daire. He couldn't dream of dragging her away to Salem County.

Yet hadn't her aunt left her a fortune in order for her to provide herself with a husband? The aunt must have realized that her family would forever keep Susan with them, fetching and carrying, helping with the children and replacing the unreliable maid, until she was a spinster beyond a marriageable age. And her parents, if not her siblings, seemed interested in him as a prospect.

But she did not have a heart for the Lord. Not that his heart felt completely at peace. He was still a wastrel, which was surely not God's will for his life. He needed a purpose, something to make him worthy of his family's love and respect.

He needed to find the goldfinch before he took time to think about his future.

With that in mind, he made his way back to Heath's office near the harbor.

The older man met Daire with a broad grin and out-stretched hands. "Come in, lad. So good to see you. May I fetch you something to drink?"

"No thank you." Daire stood in front of the chair a lackey set behind him. "I won't be here long."

"I'm sorry to hear that." With a gesture, Heath sent his assistants from the room. "Lucinda said you two had a rather unpleasant conversation last evening. I'm sorry I missed it." He chuckled deep in his thick chest. "Not the unpleasantness. I'm sure I could have smoothed things over if I'd been there."

"How did you find out about the formula?" Daire demanded.

"Ah, the formula." Heath raised a glass of amber liquid to his lips, though noon had just arrived, later than Daire wanted, the earliest Heath would see him, too early for the man's sort of drink. "Everyone knows the Balmoral crystal is special. I've been trying to get the formula for years."

"But you only export glass sometimes." Daire hooked his hands together behind his back. "You don't make it."

"No, but many a glasshouse here and in Europe would pay for that formula and the queen's favor instead of that paltry business of your family's."

"But how did you know it is in the goldfinch?" Daire asked.

Heath grinned. "Not all of your apprentices are as loyal as you would like to think they are. A little pocket money, and they are happy to write me of any upheavals at Grassicks'."

"Indeed."

Daire would have to telegraph his family and warn them of a spy in their midst.

"By the time I knew you were trying to sell it," Heath continued, "you'd pawned it off on some stranger and left town."

"So you don't know where it is?" Daire hoped he didn't sound too eager.

"I've offered some true land deals to half a dozen men in the tenements if they can get their hands on it, but none have come through." Heath snorted. "Too lazy to really work the land, I expect. They want gold for little work."

"Most of their families were farmers before the famine forced them to come here." Daire jumped to the ready defense of the city's poorest people. "And most of them are honest despite being poor and wouldn't steal."

He shot Heath a glare from beneath half-lowered lids.

Heath let out a booming laugh. "I caught that arrow straight to the heart. But it won't stop me from trying. I will have that formula if it's the last possession I gain."

"And I will stop you from ruining my family if it's the last thing I do."

Daire walked out on Heath, the man's laughter echoing in his ears.

This was Heath's city. He knew too many men in all walks of life, from the poorest to the wealthiest, the least important to the most influential. His chances of tracking down the goldfinch ran higher than Daire's. Heath had sent out the word that he would give land to any man who obtained the formula. That gave him the advantage of many potential leads.

Daire had but one.

Heart pounding as though he ran all the way, Daire approached Susan's house. No one answered his knock. He caught no glimpse of even Gran in the front window. No boys played in the back garden. The dwelling was the quietest he'd ever seen it. Quiet and too neat.

Uneasiness sent him knocking on the kitchen door and circling the premises more than once. It wasn't right for this home of boisterous, untidy, yet friendly and giving people to be silent. The large lot needed to be full of children playing. Gran should be sitting in her window drawing her insights into the family. Susan should be rushing about, her hair and a frill on her gown trailing behind her.

The image sent Daire's heart plummeting into his middle. If he didn't need Susan's help once again, he would have fled right then and there. He couldn't have such strong feelings for her. He'd made many mistakes over the years, but falling for Susan Morris would not be one of them.

Jaw set, he returned to downtown and strolled around a park, where nursemaids watched over babies and old men dozed over newspapers. When numbers boys began to fill up the open green, Daire returned to the Morris house. Surely the two boys would be long since home and someone would be there to meet them.

Once again, the house lay in unnatural silence. Daire paced around and around and around until a neighbor stepped onto her front porch and demanded to know what he was about.

"None of them are home," he said. "Do you know where they've gone?"

"You can look at the church." The woman's smooth face creased into a frown. "It has been quiet there today. I hope nothing's wrong."

"So do I." Daire started to let himself out of the gate.

"Don't you want to know which church?" the woman called after him.

"I already know." Daire waved to her and quickened his pace.

The church lay only a few blocks away. He hoped that someone there would know the whereabouts of at least one of the Morrises, and they all hadn't been mislaid, as Sam had been.

Daire smiled at the notion, where he would have been disgusted just the other day. The Morrises weren't uncaring. He'd seen how they worried. They simply kept their minds focused on others so much they tended to forget what was under their noses.

At the church entrance, he heard the sound of female voices and started in that direction. But he passed the sanctuary on the way, and its quiet dimness drew him in, called to him to stop and do more than hope. He'd told Susan that true hope came from God, yet he hadn't asked for it himself. He'd been trusting in his own devices to find the goldfinch in order to save his family, in order to make himself acceptable to them again. But what of putting his hope, his future, in God and being acceptable to Him?

He talked and thought a great deal about faith in God, even repented of his months with the Heaths. He had not, however, since leaving home, focused on anything beyond finding the goldfinch, trying not to be attracted to Susan Morris, and being able to return triumphant to his family. The safety of his family, where being a Christian, or at least living like one, was easy.

"And I criticize her for not being a Christian." He dropped onto one of the pews and closed his eyes. "Lord, I am failing on my own once again, yet if I do not find the goldfinch, I can't go home. I can't face them. Please let me find it."

He believed God could help him find the ornament with its precious contents, yet peace eluded him. The swell of female voices grew louder, as though they approached, and he scrambled to his feet, afraid they would leave before he finished his devotion or worked out why finally asking for God's help in finding the goldfinch didn't make him feel better.

Neither did seeing Mrs. Morris leading the pack of ladies toward the church entrance, her three eldest daughters following in her wake like ducklings.

"Mr. Grassick." She stopped and gave him her brilliant smile. "What a pleasure to see you here. But if you've come to meet Deborah, I'm afraid she's spoken for." She laughed.

Daire felt warm under his collar. "I, um, am actually looking for Miss Susan."

"Susan?" Mrs. Morris looked blank. "She never comes to help us here. We need her at home."

"She isn't there," Daire said.

"She's gone with the boys to find our maid, Bridget McCorkle," Deborah informed him. "Remember, Momma? We didn't want another cold supper."

"Oh yes. I was so occupied with the bazaar I completely forgot. Didn't my mother tell you where to find Susan?"

Her mother? Oh, that must be Gran.

"She wasn't there either," Daire said.

The four Morris ladies' faces registered shock.

"Where could she be?" Mrs. Morris wailed. "Mother never goes anywhere."

"She probably just didn't come to the door," Daisy murmured, patting her mother's arm. "We'll all go to the house and find everyone safely there."

"Allow me to escort you." Daire offered his arm to Mrs. Morris.

She took it, and her hand shook a little. "Susan should be home by now, too."

"I'm sure they all will be, ma'am."

At least he hoped they were.

But no one was, except for Gran. Moving with the slowness of a giant turtle, Gran tottered around the kitchen, leaning against the worktable or gripping the handle of the oven door, as she appeared to prepare supper—and to do well with it, judging from the delicious aroma of stew wafting through the house.

"Mother, you're cooking." Mrs. Morris's eyes widened. "You haven't cooked for twenty years."

"That's twenty years too long." Gran chuckled. "At least in the summer, when the arthritis isn't so bad. But someone had to do it. Susan tried. She left stew simmering earlier—"

"Susan!" the ladies cried.

"She doesn't know how to cook," Opal said.

"She was trying," Gran explained. "But when she didn't come home soon enough, it started to burn, so I got Mr. Lamb to take me to the market in his buggy for fresh provisions and started over."

"Why?" was all anyone could seem to ask.

"I was afraid once Susan knew how to cook, none of you would ever let her go get herself a husband." Gran stirred the kettle on the stove. "She wants to make you all so happy she would give up her own happiness to ensure yours. And I couldn't let that happen, even if—" She cast a pleading glance at Daire. "Will you help an old lady to that chair?"

He saw the lines of pain then, etching deep grooves on either side of her mouth.

If Susan saw what her grandmother suffered for her sake, she would never doubt that at least one member of her family loved her and cherished her.

"I can carry you into the parlor if you prefer, ma'am," he offered.

"No, the kitchen chair will do." She clasped his arm. "Someone needs to supervise."

"I can cook." Opal rushed to the stove. "William gives the maid two days a week off, and I do for us on those days."

"Where is Susan?" Deborah asked. "She should be home by now."

"And the boys." Mrs. Morris fluttered her long, narrow hands in front of her. "The boys should have come home by now, too. They just had to go find Bridget."

Hairs along the back of Daire's neck rose. "How long ago would they have gone?"

"Two hours and more," Gran said. "They left as soon as the boys returned from school."

"Left for where?" He kept his tone even with effort.

"To find our maid." Mrs. Morris's eyes had reddened, as though she were trying not to cry. "I know where she lives and her surname, so I sent Susan and the boys to find her. I was so sure they'd be all right in the daylight. But two hours is far too long."

"Where would they have gone?" Daire headed for the door. "I'll go."

"I'll go with you." Deborah followed him.

"But Gerrit is coming over shortly," Daisy said.

"He can wait if he has a mind to." Deborah tossed her head. "My little sister needs me."

"Do you know where to go?" Daire asked.

"I know the name of the street." Deborah made a face. "Maybe we can find that."

"I expect we can."

"If we know where to start."

Back at the tenements, Daire stared where a group of boys played a boisterous game with balls and sticks. He was about to lead Deborah around them when he caught sight of the youngest Morris boy jumping up and down on the sidelines.

"Paul," Deborah cried.

He turned, caught sight of her, and tried to duck in front of two bigger boys.

Daire lunged forward and caught him by the shirt collar. "Stop right there, young man." He drew Paul from the crowd. "You are supposed to be with Susan. Where is she?"

"She's not here?" Paul glanced around.

"Paul." Deborah loomed over him, her face tight. "You were supposed to accompany Susan here to Bridget's, not play ball. Where is she? And where is Roger?"

"Roger's there." Paul pointed his thumb to the center of the circled spectators.

Roger swung a stick at a flying ball. *Thwack.* The connection of ball and stick sounded over cheers.

"He's so good," Paul said on a sigh. "If I were taller—"

"Susan," Daire interrupted.

Paul stuck out his lower lip. "I don't know. We got invited to play and—er—sort of forgot about her."

"Don't we all." Deborah shook her head. "Do you think she's gone off to find Bridget on her own?"

Daire glanced around the street. "Since she's not here and not at home, we can only hope that's where she is. I should say *pray* where she is," he added.

"All right." Paul squirmed in Daire's hold. "Can I return to the game?"

"No, you cannot." Daire glanced at Deborah. "Will you hold him while I retrieve the other one? Roger, is it?"

"Yes and yes." Deborah clamped her hand onto Paul's collar in Daire's place. "Don't move, little brother. If you so much as blink, I'll. . ."

Daire didn't hear the rest of the threat as he shouldered his way through the youths, enduring a number of unpleasant names directed at him, and found Roger as his comrades shouted him back to where he'd hit the ball.

"Take your bow and leave," Daire commanded.

"Who are—oh, Mr. Grassick." Roger mopped his sweaty face with a shirtsleeve. "What're you doing here?"

"Looking for the sister you seem to have mislaid."

"Susan? She's not here?" Roger glanced around as Paul had.

"No, she's not." Daire resisted the urge to shake the lad. It wouldn't have been right or fair. He knew the lure of a ball game and friends. Roger should have obeyed his parents and stayed with Susan, and that was his parents' place to correct him for his actions. He should have called on Susan earlier instead of abandoning her because he didn't have the strength to resist a lady's attractions.

"We'll go find her now," he said in a calmer tone.

"All right." Roger called a farewell to his companions, receiving many protests in return, and followed Daire back to where Deborah still gripped Paul.

"We need to find someone to direct us to this Mulberry Street," Daire said.

"There's a hundred people around," Paul pointed out. "Ask any of them."

Daire chose a young woman with two small children clinging to her skirt and a baby in her arms. In response, she held out her hand. Daire gave her a quarter, and she gave them directions.

"Left, then right, then right again. . ."

All of them lost the directions after the fourth turn. They stopped an old man, who demanded four bits for his trouble. Daire gave him a quarter instead of fifty cents then gave another quarter to an urchin in a clean shirt and short pants with a dirty face.

A dollar later, they reached the whitewashed door a neighbor assured them belonged to the flat of Bridget McCorkle. The portal stood open onto dimly lit rooms.

"Should we go in?" Paul whispered.

"We won't find anyone standing in the street," Roger retorted.

"We'll knock first," Deborah suggested.

Knocking produced nothing more than a few curious glances from people in other doorways and one old lady's information that Bridget might be in the courtyard.

"How do we get to the courtyard?" Daire asked.

"Go on through," the woman told them. "She won't mind,

least I didn't hear her complaining about the young lady earlier."

"Susan," the three Morrises and Daire said together.

Daire held out an arm to bar the boys from charging through the flat, though he wished to do the same himself. At a sedate pace, Deborah's skirts swishing over the bare floorboards, they tramped through the narrow, dark rooms of the flat until reaching the rear door. It, too, stood open. Beyond it, the courtyard teemed with life, everyone in constant motion except for a young lady in a crumpled blue dress, who sat on the pavement with one of her maple syrup–colored curls clutched in the hand of a laughing baby.

Gazing at the image of Susan holding a child in her arms, Daire couldn't remember why he'd wanted to stay away from her.

"I never knew she was so beautiful," Deborah murmured.

"She's that and more," Daire responded in an awed voice. "I think—"

"There's Bridget!" Paul shouted.

Daire jumped and swung toward where the boy pointed. Half a dozen middle-aged matrons gathered around a cooking pot.

"Which one?" he asked.

"That one." Paul raced forward. "Bridget, we've been looking for you."

"Aye, and you found me." One woman detached herself from the others and trudged forward. "But you shouldn't have been sending Miss Susan here on her own. She's been here for hours, caring for the little ones while we got some washing up done."

"We've come for her now," Daire said. "But you could have gotten her home."

"Aye, I could have, but she wouldn't leave." Bridget glared at him from brilliant dark eyes. "Not that you'll be believing me. You'll be saying I've kept her here against her will."

Daire glanced at Susan, who was gazing at them but not moving.

"Why would you think that I'd have such uncharitable thoughts about you?" he asked.

"Because I took your goldfinch bottle," Bridget confessed.

twelve

Susan couldn't move. The child in her arms had finally stopped crying after she'd sent an older boy running for some milky mush to feed the little one. His mother had died the day before, and the distraught father didn't know what to do, so he left the boy in charge of the other children. They couldn't spare much food from the mouths of their own children for the baby, so he wailed with hunger until mere pennies from Susan gave him enough sustenance to quiet him down.

As long as she continued to hold him.

When Bridget returned to the courtyard, Susan couldn't approach her. With the child in her arms, she couldn't get to her feet, and she feared setting him down might get him trampled. Moreover, after the way he had displayed the power of his lungs the other two times she'd tried to relinquish her hold on him, she feared he would throw another fit.

Bridget didn't come to Susan, though their eyes met across the courtyard. Suspicion turned to certainty over the maid's part in the goldfinch's disappearance. Otherwise, she would have spoken, demanding what Susan was doing there, if nothing else.

Susan wished she could see Daire's face as he talked to Bridget. Hers was stony, cold. His stance was rigid.

He'd been taut since he stepped out of Bridget's flat and caught sight of Susan. She hadn't looked at him directly, but she caught the flash of tenderness in his face, a softening that made her heart feel like mush, before he turned his back on her and marched toward Bridget with shoulders as rigid as a building wall.

Such nice shoulders.

"I love him," Susan murmured to the baby.

He cooed in response and took two fistfuls of her hair.

"But he'll never love me. He'll get his goldfinch back and leave."

The baby giggled.

Smiling, Susan cuddled him close. "I can live without him if I can make babies like you laugh."

If she could bring hope to the little ones and their parents.

"How can I do this, Lord? I don't know You enough to talk to people like Deborah talked to me, but I must do. . . something."

Her gaze strayed to Daire. Her heart had reformed itself from the ball of mush and now bounced off the wall of her chest like a ball. It hurt to have him ignore her. Physically hurt.

"There, Lord, I have no hope."

As though he felt the intensity of her gaze, Daire turned his head and looked at her. Saying something to Bridget that Susan couldn't hear, he crossed the courtyard and stooped before Susan. "We were worried about you."

"I was worried about me, too, for a while." Susan stared at him with her feelings bursting forth. "Then I helped with this little one, and I forgot about being lost and Bridget and your goldfinch." She glanced down. "Did she take it?"

"Yes." Daire held out his hands. "I'll help you up and you can hear what she has to say for herself."

"You aren't going to have her arrested?"

"I should." Daire's mouth went grim. "But I doubt I will. Now, how do we manage this if you won't let go of that baby?"

"Maybe Deborah can hold him for a minute."

They called for Deborah to join them. The boys trailing behind her, she crossed the courtyard to where Susan sat. She took the child, who immediately started to wail. Daire assisted

Susan to her feet. He didn't let go of her hands as soon as she stood but remained holding them in a firm, warm grip, while he smiled down at her, an odd expression on his face, as though he didn't recognize her and thought he should.

"Bridget," Susan said in a breathless voice.

"This baby is making a scene," Deborah piped up.

Daire dropped Susan's hands as though they'd turned into hot pokers, and she took the child from Deborah.

"I don't know what to do with him," she admitted. "His father has gone off to find work, and he doesn't have a mamma now, poor thing. The baby, not the father."

"I doubt anyone will notice if you take him home." Deborah laughed to show she wasn't serious.

"Since he's quiet now," Daire said, "can we think of his future after we talk some sense into Bridget?"

"You won't get sense out of her," Deborah predicted. "She's adamant."

"About what?" Susan asked.

"Not telling us where the goldfinch is," Daire grumbled. "She took it, but I can't even persuade her to sell it back to me."

"Why not?" Susan glowered at the woman who had been their maid for nearly a year. "Bridget, why won't you sell the goldfinch back to Mr. Grassick?"

"It isn't his to buy back," Bridget answered. "Nor mine to sell," she added.

Behind her, the other women drew away, turning their backs on Bridget. Space encircled the Morrises, Daire, and Bridget. Beyond the gap, the courtyard fell silent. Those who remained watched and listened in silence.

Feeling as though she performed on a stage, Susan moved closer to Bridget. "No, the goldfinch isn't Mr. Grassick's. It's mine, and I will give it back to him. This piece is important to his family."

"So important he sold it on the street?" Bridget curled her upper lip. "And you shoved it into a corner to do nothing but collect dust? Well, now it's important to my son."

"You have a son?" Susan blurted out the words before she realized the possible consequences.

Bridget slapped her hands onto her hips. "You see me nearly every day for a year, and you don't ask my surname. You don't know where I live. You don't know I have a son, who wants to be married if he can prove to his girl's family he's good enough for them. But he won't be doing that without the work, will he?"

"How can he do it with the goldfinch?" Daire asked in an exaggeratedly calm manner.

"He'll sell it to Leonard Heath," Bridget said. "Then he'll have land and money to get a new start."

"And you'd let him do that at the expense of Mr. Grassick's family?" Susan demanded so harshly the baby whimpered.

"They have land already," Bridget reasoned. "A man can have hope if he has land to work and a future."

"Will his conscience let him enjoy his prosperity?" Deborah spoke in gentle tones. "Mr. Grassick and Susan may have discarded the goldfinch because they thought it held little monetary value at the time, but that doesn't change the fact that you stole it. We could have you arrested."

"You won't find it here or nowhere," Bridget declared.

"No, but we all heard you confess to taking it," Deborah continued.

"There's no proof," Bridget insisted.

"She's right," Daire said. "For all we know, her son took it and she's lying for him."

"I thought you were a Christian, Bridget," Paul spoke up in a sullen voice. "You always prayed with us at meals."

"Aye, and I prayed that God would provide for my son, and there was that bottle setting there with no one caring a whit for what happened to it."

"You can't buy hope," Susan said. "I'm an heiress. I can have all the stuff I like, but my heart is still lacking something I know only comes from God, if I can figure out how." She added the last bit under her breath.

Daire shot her a quick glance then returned his attention to Bridget. "At least let me talk to your son."

"I can't be doing that." Bridget's face worked, and tears brightened her eyes. "You'll be having him arrested if he has the goldfinch in his possession."

"I won't." Daire sighed. "Mrs. McCorkle, I just want my property back."

"Aye, and when you get it, my son will have naught."

"I can—" Daire stopped, and his features twisted as though he were in pain. "I can't make him promises, ma'am, but if you keep him from selling the goldfinch to Leonard Heath for a week, I'll work out a fair exchange for him."

"All right, then." Bridget folded her hands across her middle. "I'll be doing that—if it's not too late."

❧

"I have to go home," Daire announced.

He stood on the walk in front of the Morris house with Susan, who still held the baby bundled in her shawl. The other Morrises had vanished inside the instant the front gate opened, leaving him alone with Susan.

He gazed down at her, his heart heavier than it should have been with the hope of retrieving the goldfinch before Heath, still holding life.

"I don't have the resources to persuade Bridget's son to sell me the goldfinch," he explained, though his neck felt hot with the humiliation of admitting that he, a man of twenty-five, still depended on his family for his income. "I should have money. They've given me enough over the years. . . ."

"And mine is secured away from me, or I'd give it to you for being the cause of so much trouble for you and your family." Susan's eyes glowed in the dying light of the day. "I wanted to give it to this baby's father so he didn't have to abandon his son. If I—"

"I'll work for my family at anything and earn it back," Daire broke in. "It's beyond time I stopped being irresponsible and took my place in the family business."

"Even if you don't want that?"

"I want to be with my family. The city. . ." He gazed past her shoulder, away from the heart-melting sight of her cuddling an increasingly fussy baby. "I've done nothing but make mistakes here."

"Then—then you won't come back?" Her voice broke only a little, but from the corner of his eye, he caught the glint of a tear on her cheek.

"I can't."

One reason was that a mere five more minutes in her company and he would do something ungentlemanly and foolish, like kiss her right there in front of her family home and all the neighbors. In no way could he make that sort of a commitment. She didn't share his faith in God, and even if she found a relationship with the Lord, she had just reminded him that she was an heiress. If he married her, he would simply go from depending on his family for his daily bread to depending on his wife. He would never learn to make responsible decisions for himself.

"How will you get the goldfinch back from Mr. McCorkle if you stay away?" Susan asked.

"I'll send up one of my brothers, or even my grandfather." He managed a smile. "Grandfather is a formidable figure."

"Isn't that having your family help you out of a scrape again?"

Daire winced at the truth of her words.

"I can't help but think," Susan continued, shifting so he couldn't avoid meeting her gaze, "that if you're putting your hope for your future in God, you could find out what is right for your life no matter where you live, with or without your family to protect you."

He opened his mouth to object, and nothing emerged.

Surely she misunderstood something. At the moment, he couldn't think what, though he wished to believe she was wrong.

"I'll ponder that," he compromised. "And what will you do with that baby?"

"I'll take care of him until someone can be found to do so. My family won't care. They love children, and all the women near Bridget's flat know I have him. Someone will send word if the father comes seeking him."

"I'll pray for you, Miss Susan." He laid his forefinger along the baby's smooth cheek. "And this one."

"Thank you. I'll practice praying by praying for you." She smiled, though more tears trickled down her face.

"Don't despair." Daire brushed them away. "God will show you what He wants for you."

"I already know," Susan said. "What I need from God is for Him to make the bankers give me control of my money." She turned her head and kissed his fingertips. "Good-bye, Daire Grassick. I won't give up looking for your goldfinch."

❧

"Nor will I give up on you," she whispered to his retreating figure.

With the baby fussing, she blinked tears from her eyes and headed for the house. Deborah had already prepared the family for the new arrival, and Momma had everything set up in the nursery.

"You can't keep him, though," she said. "You're too young and without a husband. It wouldn't look right."

"I know. He needs his father." Susan spooned mush into the baby's mouth. "His father needs him, too. I could see how much it hurt him to leave his son with me, a stranger, but he couldn't afford his flat and needed to work and—Momma?"

"Yes?" Momma paused at the nursery door.

"Do you think Daddy can tell me how I can break the trust Great-aunt Morris set up for my inheritance?"

"Of course he can. He's an excellent banker, for all his dreamy poet's heart." Her smile held tenderness. "Would you like me to send him in?"

"If he doesn't mind the baby."

"Your father mind? My dear, he loves babies. Have you never read the poems he's written about all of you as infants?"

"No." Susan bowed her head. "I've read very little of his poetry." She'd thought it merely a personal amusement, much like Gran drawing caricatures purely for her own enjoyment.

"I'll give you the notebook he wrote for you." Momma left Susan.

A few moments later, her father arrived and settled himself on a chair adjacent to Susan's. "You're doing a good thing there, Susan, taking in that poor orphaned child."

"It's only temporary, but someone needed to do it, and I was the only person who could. I have the resources to take care of him, at least for a while." She leaned toward her father. "I want more resources. There's a man named Leonard Heath who lures young men west with promises of land if they work for him for a while in his mines and on his railroad. But they never earn enough to get the land, or even to come back here, because they hardly get any wages. People here are finding out the truth of his plans, and they're wary of accepting them, but they don't have hope for anything else if there's no work on the docks." She paused for breath.

"I know of Heath. We can't seem to stop him, as much as we'd like to. He has some powerful friends in high places. But what does this have to do with your trust?"

"I want to break it. I want to start a mission that will help people resettle farther west, where there's land and work. I haven't quite thought of how I'll do this, but I want the money to try."

"Hmm." Her father tapped his toe on the carpeted floor. "You want to do something similar to Heath's work, but honestly."

"Yes." Susan patted the baby's back. "Is it possible?"

"Not unless you marry," he said. "I'll talk to your trustees tomorrow, and from what I recall, that is the only way you gain control of your money."

"Control if my husband allows me to spend it." Susan ground her teeth in frustration. "And what husband will want to spend it on other people?"

"The right one, my dear. The right one."

That right one was definitely not Daire Grassick. But, oh, how her heart hurt over his leaving.

Oddly, reading her father's poetry helped soothe her pain over Daire leaving. The verses weren't terribly good, as their meter was uneven and the rhymes often forced. Yet the sentiment and emotion behind each line told Susan that he didn't in the least ignore his children's presence. On the contrary, he loved every one of them and his grandchildren.

He's shy, she thought. *Like me.*

The baby cooed at the sound of her voice.

"You should be sleeping, young man."

He slept soon and woke hungry. Susan fed him, got herself ready for the day, and set out for the tenements. She didn't have more than her pin money to use to ease the plight of the people there, but she had time and willing hands. She used both for half of each day, watching children for weary mothers, cooking or fetching and carrying for infirm elderly persons, and always seeking Bridget McCorkle's son.

On the third day there, she learned that his name was Daniel, a good, hardworking young man, who wanted to marry the daughter of a ship's purser.

"He'll do anything to win her father's approval," gradually trusting ladies admitted.

"I understand," Susan said.

She had taken some foolish steps to win her family's attention, if not their approval, from buying the goldfinch to show them she understood pretty things, to dashing about the city with Daire and Deborah to find Sam. Deborah had gone along to make Gerrit jealous enough to propose at last, and Susan had lost her heart to Daire.

Gerrit proposed to Deborah after church on Wednesday night, and Susan was the first person to learn the happy news.

She hadn't been able to keep Daire in the city, but she had become friends with her sister and gained an understanding of her own abilities.

She couldn't sew or persuade people to donate money to good causes. She couldn't even use her own money to support those causes. But she could bring a smile to a weary woman's face by washing her clothes so she could rest, and she could sing small children to sleep. Her new charge went with her everywhere. She wanted to ensure the father would know where his son was so he could find him. In the meantime, she tried to find a family willing to take on another responsibility for the little bit of money she could give them from the allowance the bankers permitted. Thus far, everyone said his father's or mother's family should take on the responsibility of caring for the boy. So, each day, carrying the little one, whom she had taken to calling Frankie, she went home weary and often dirty, and so joyful it masked the hurt of Daire leaving.

Going to church on Sunday reminded her of being there with Daire and the sermon on the lost lamb. She sat in the pew, reading the previous week's lesson in Luke, and her heart opened to the fullness of understanding. She was like the lost lamb, and God cared so much about her, He had led her into the fold. "Please forgive me for not following You sooner," she prayed under her breath. "I accept You into my life."

She still wanted her family's approval. She still longed for a husband who would not want her inheritance to line his pockets, but to do good in the world. She prayed she would find the goldfinch so Daire would return and she could share her newfound faith with him. And she now knew God had been paying attention to her all along, that He was interested in even the least of her actions. As she hoped, He provided, for He was the source of all hope.

For the first time, she stood and sang the hymns with her heart, not caring if her voice soared above the others. She sang to the Lord, not to gain attention.

"What a blessing your singing was," an elderly lady told Susan as they exited the sanctuary. "Why have we never heard you sing before?"

"I never felt God's Spirit in my soul before." Susan wanted to skip out of the church and tell the whole world.

She settled for her family. "I finally understand," she announced at dinner. "God cares about me as much as anyone, and He will provide me with the right husband if I'm supposed to have one."

"We'll help introduce you to nice young men," Opal pronounced. "As soon as we find another maid for Momma."

"I did hope it would be that nice Grassick boy," Momma said. "I thought he showed some interest in you the other day when he was so distraught about you not being home."

"He wants his family more," Susan said, gazing at her plate. "He doesn't care for the city."

"Then he doesn't care enough about you to deserve you," Deborah declared. "We'll find someone else, now that you seem ready to marry."

"I'll wait." Susan cocked her head. "Frankie is crying. Please excuse me."

"What will you do with him?" Momma asked. "You can't keep him."

Susan stood. "I'm praying his father comes back."

The child's father came back that Thursday. He tracked Susan down in one of the courtyards, where she was reading the story of Noah to a group of children and mothers pretending not to listen.

"I'll be taking my son now." He held out his hands.

Trying not to feel a little resentment that he would just snatch Frankie away from her without a by-your-leave, since the child was his, Susan scrambled to her feet and scooped Frankie from his nest of blankets. "You found work?" The question was brazen, perhaps even rude, and she wanted to ensure the baby would be cared for.

"Aye, I'm going to sea." The way the young man drew his son against his chest brought tears to Susan's eyes, his love was so apparent.

Yet alarm tightened her chest. "He's too little to go to sea, sir."

"He won't. I'm marrying his mother's cousin before I ship out."

"Is she—can she...?" Aware of their audience, Susan decided not to ask if the new wife was old enough to take care of the boy.

She twisted her hands in the apron she'd taken to wearing. "May I still call on him?"

"If you like." The young man's features softened. "I know I owe you for taking him in like you done."

"No sir, you don't. I was happy—"

"I don't take charity." His strong chin jutted forward. "I haven't the coin, but I have the information you're wanting."

"Information?" Susan held her breath, not daring to speculate or hope.

"Aye, I know where you can find Daniel McCorkle."

thirteen

"I've failed." Daire faced his entire family for his confession. "I couldn't find the goldfinch, and by now, Leonard Heath has it." He made himself look his grandfather in the eye. "I'm sorry. I've helped that greedy, dishonest man destroy your life's work."

"I knew we never should have—"

"Jock," Jordan interrupted the youngest brother. "Leave off. Daire had a right to take the goldfinch."

"It's my fault for putting the formula in it in the first place." Maggie screwed up her face, and tears glistened in her eyes.

Maggie never cried. Daire remembered thinking that when Susan had burst into tears in her kitchen. Now Maggie held her serviette to her face and sniffed.

"Twice in one week," he muttered.

"Twice what?" Jordan asked.

"I've made a lady cry." Daire glanced toward his grandparents and parents. "Have you nothing to say to me? Will things be so bad that I can't beg you all to hire me on as an accountant or something menial like sweeping up the cullet?"

"You'd probably cut yourself on the cullet," Jock muttered.

Daire shot him an impatient glance. Only the most incompetent of people would cut themselves on the pieces of glass let to fall onto the glassworks floor as the glassblowers snipped and shaped the cooling glass.

"I've a great deal to say to you, lad," Grandfather spoke, his Scots burr thick. "You should not be making the ladies weep."

"What other lady?" Maggie demanded, her own tears drying in an instant.

"Well, um—" Daire squirmed on his dining room chair. His neck cloth felt too tight. "Miss Susan Morris, the young lady who bought the goldfinch from me."

"Why did you make her cry?" Grandmomma asked.

"I took her into the tenements." While the family drank tea or coffee, according to personal preference, and ate scones and other delicacies in the afternoon tea Grandmomma had taken to while in London seven years earlier, Daire recounted the tale of his days in Hudson City.

"And you just left her there?" Maggie cried. "Daire, you dolt, you nodcock, you—"

"That's enough," Father broke in, his voice quiet, firm. "Daire made a wise decision if the young lady doesn't know if she's a Christian or not."

"But what if she becomes one?" Maggie persisted. "He's thrown away someone who sounds perfectly lovely—"

"She's an heiress," Daire announced.

A moment of silence reigned over the table; then Jock said, "She can save the company after the queen sues us for breach of contract."

"What is wrong with being an heiress?" Grandmomma demanded.

She had been an heiress herself, a fact that stood in her and Grandfather's way of happiness for a while.

"I don't think—" Daire looked from Jock, to Jordan, to Maggie.

"We won't leave," Maggie declared. "We worried about you while you were gone, just as much as anyone else, so we have a right to know."

"I'll make Jock behave himself." Jordan shot a playful punch in his younger brother's direction. "Can you keep your trap shut?"

"I suppose." Jock sighed, but the glance he sent in Daire's direction held compassion. "I can make some guesses about our proud big brother."

"I'm not—" Daire blinked and began to turn his coffee cup around on its saucer. "It's more than pride."

"Is it?" Grandfather asked. "If the young lady were a Christian, would you still have left her behind?"

Daire stared at the whirling liquid in his cup until he thought his eyes would cross. In each shimmer of afternoon sunlight off the brew, he thought he saw Susan's face, her purplish blue eyes shimmering in the daylight—sparkling with joy. Sparkling with tears. Sparkling with an emotion he understood she directed at him.

"Does this heiress care for you?" Momma asked.

Daire nodded without looking up.

"Was she seeking the Lord," Grandfather inquired, "or was she more like Miss Heath?"

"She was nothing like Lucinda." Daire's head shot up. "Susan is lovely and sweet and kind and shy and—"

His family's laughter drowned out his acclaim of Susan's virtues.

"Then why didn't you make her an offer and bring her down here to meet us?" Jock demanded.

"Or invite us up to meet her?" Jordan added.

"Her family needs her, and I'm not sure of her faith, and—"

"You're thinking you have naught to offer her," Grandfather concluded.

"I don't even have my inheritance or share from the glassworks if the formula is truly lost," Daire confirmed.

"Is she interested in you?" Jock asked.

"I—yes." Daire welcomed the cool breeze through the open windows.

"And is it your connections to us or your money she's wanting?" Grandfather pressed.

"I—don't believe so." Daire spoke with caution, not certain what Grandfather intended.

"Then 'tis you that attracts her," Grandfather pressed.

"I have reason to believe so," Daire admitted in a tone

that sounded hoarse. He swallowed a drink of coffee. "But it doesn't matter. She lives in the city, and I live down here. She wants to work with the poor in the city, and I want to remain here, where—where—"

No, he wouldn't admit that much in front of his siblings.

"Besides, none of it matters, now that I've lost the goldfinch."

Silence fell over the table, save for a bee that had flown through one of the windows and hovered over the jam pots, buzzing.

"If you had found the goldfinch," Father posed, "would you have considered pursuing a courtship of this young woman?"

"Yes," Daire responded without hesitation.

"Then that settles it." Grandfather snapped his handkerchief through the air and captured the bee against the table cloth. "I created the goldfinch as a gift for the lady I love, not as a possession to cause strife and heartache in the family I love. Now 'tis coming between you and your brother and sister, and you and the lady you love, and you and God; we need to all confess that we've made an object too important to us."

"But the formula," Maggie burst out. "Grandfather, it's more than the goldfinch we're looking for. It's the formula."

"And the contract with Queen Victoria to always be able to produce her crystal," Jock added. "You know we will be ruined without it."

"And if we're putting our financial security above our happiness, or worse, our relationship with the Lord," Grandfather said in his sonorous voice, "then 'tis past time we gave it up."

Daire opened his mouth to argue. From the corners of his eyes, he saw his siblings and even his grandmother struggling with the same impulse. Momma and Father, like Grandfather, sat motionless with peaceful faces.

Mouth dry, Daire snatched up the handkerchief still trapping the bee and carried it to the window. Gently, he lowered the cloth over the sill and drew the fabric away. The bee lay on a rhododendron leaf for a moment as though stunned; then its wings fluttered and it soared toward the nearby rosebushes.

"Even the bees have a purpose in their lives," he murmured, more to himself than anyone. Then he turned his face up to the clear blue sky and spoke with more firmness. "My life was centered around proving myself good at something so you all would care about me, but I didn't succeed, and you all still care. Then I failed to get the goldfinch and formula back, and yet you continue to care, to love me. Now I just need to have something to do with my life, and if the glassworks will perhaps fail, you won't need me to keep the books and take orders, or even clean up cullet. I haven't been very good at getting through life on my own." He faced them. "Will you help me?"

"It's past time you asked, son," Father said. "What would you like help with? And I'll start by asking you what you've prayed for besides help with finding the goldfinch."

"I—well, I. . ." Daire held his father's gaze. "Nothing. I simply ran back to you all each time I didn't succeed at something."

"We're happy to have you home." Momma held her hands out to him. "But you've never found your niche here, which tells me you're supposed to be somewhere else."

"Not that we're telling you to leave again," Jock put in. "Not even me."

Daire's heart warmed and swelled until his chest tightened.

"You haven't the aptitude for the glassmaking or the farming," Grandfather pointed out. "So we've always thought the Lord had something else planned for you."

"*Therefore shall a man leave his father and his mother.*" Maggie quoted from Genesis in a whisper loud enough to be heard from a stage.

"We hoped you'd find it in your wanderings," Grandmomma said.

"But I never did." Daire met each of his family members' eyes. "My carelessness and wanderings cost this family dearly. How can God have a plan for me now?"

"He does," Grandfather said. "But you thought you failed us, so you've run back here to hide, but you won't be hiding from what the Lord wants for you and have the peace in your heart. Now, if you all will be excusing me, I am going to the glasshouse to mix the crystal formula as I recall it."

"Grandfather." Maggie leaped to her feet. "I'm certain you're adding too much quartz—" She dashed after her long-legged grandfather.

"So what do you plan to do, Daire?" Jock challenged.

Daire smiled. "A lot of praying."

And a lot of walking.

Summer's sticky heat hadn't yet descended upon southern New Jersey. Daire took advantage of the warm sunshine and coolness beneath the towering pine trees to walk and think. He tried to focus on praying, on asking God what he should do now. He found himself crying out in despair that the goldfinch had remained lost, that a man like Leonard Heath would prosper.

Even if Heath's prosperity at the expense of the Grassicks meant a better life for Bridget's son, Daire couldn't understand why God would allow the wicked to win. He fought against it.

And when he wasn't struggling to accept how things worked out, he too often thought of Susan. He prayed she found her relationship with God for which she had been seeking. He thought he should pray she found the right sort of husband so she could use her fortune for the good. The words refused to come to him. His mind—and his heart—would not wrap around the notion of Susan as another man's wife.

"If I had something to offer her"—he began his daily devotional a week after returning home, as he had begun it many other times—"I could—"

The sight of Jock and his fiancée, Violet, walking hand in hand toward him, changed the course of his words.

"I could marry Susan. If only I'd found the goldfinch."

Yet what would he have done if he had found it? It wouldn't make him talented at glassmaking or interested in farming. The search for it had taken him from his family, back to the city, where he freed his mind and heart of the Heaths' tug on him, met Susan, and saw a need to help the families in the tenements, do something in opposition to Heath's swindles. With money, he could do so much good, especially with a wife interested in the same.

Especially with a wife with an inheritance.

Daire shook his head, rejecting the notion. It would be wrong, would it not?

"Only if you do not love her," Grandfather assured him later, when Daire told him of his notion. "And if 'tis what the Lord wants for you, Miss Morris will be wanting the same, I'm thinking."

"And it will make up for the loss of the goldfinch and the formula," Daire added.

"Or 'tis the reason for the missing goldfinch," Grandfather suggested.

"I'd find comfort in knowing that." Daire studied his grandfather's craggy face. "How do I go back there, face her after I simply walked away? She'll think I only want to marry her because she's an heiress."

"Nay, lad, not if she, too, is seeking the Lord's will. But don't tarry. Take one of our horses."

Daire did tarry. He kept imagining Susan rejecting his suit. She would have no use for him, a man with no prospects except for a way to spend her money for her, however much good he intended. Staying home, making himself useful wherever he could, from cleaning out stables to indeed sweeping up cullet from the glassworks floor to packing fragile pieces of glass for shipping, was safer.

And wrong for him.

He knew this. For nearly ten years, he'd left the family every chance he found. Now he wanted to stay when his family encouraged him to go. He didn't want to fail again. At the same time, no success came from hiding away. Without trusting in God to direct his steps, he would never find the purpose in life for which he'd hoped for a decade.

The Thursday after he returned home, he woke and began to pack.

"I'm leaving tomorrow," he announced at breakfast.

The telegram arrived by suppertime:

FOUND BRIDGET'S SON.

fourteen

"This is a wedding." Susan stared at the throng of people filling one of the tenement courtyards as she spoke to Deborah and Gerrit. "Frankie's father said I'd find Daniel McCorkle here."

"You will." Gerrit gestured above the heads of most of the crowd, using his height to advantage. "I believe Mr. McCorkle is the bridegroom. At least Bridget is standing beside the best-dressed man here, and a young lady is in a white dress and veil."

"But—" Susan blinked back tears.

If Daniel McCorkle was getting married already, he must have sold the goldfinch to Leonard Heath. The information from Frankie's father had come too late to help Daire.

And Daire wasn't there. She'd sent the telegram Thursday morning. This was Saturday afternoon, and she had received no response. He should have gotten there by now, if he were coming at all. Her heart ached with emptiness and now loss. Perhaps Daire not coming was for the best. Her telegram must have raised his hopes, and now the wedding would dash them again.

Unless, of course, he'd gone straight to Heath, or sent someone from his family straight to Heath, to negotiate for return of the goldfinch and formula. Perhaps the Grassicks could take legal action against Heath if they proved he had acquired the goldfinch and formula through illegal means.

"And that would get Mr. McCorkle arrested, since he stole the goldfinch," Susan mused aloud.

She doubted even Deborah and Gerrit could hear her above the fiddle music and cheers and shouts of friendly teasing erupting from the throng of merrymakers.

"His mother stole it," Deborah responded, apparently possessed of excellent hearing. "She'd be the one to be arrested."

"Her son knew it wasn't hers." Susan stood on tiptoe, craning her neck in an attempt to see the bride and groom.

She saw Daire Grassick instead. He stood on the other side of the courtyard, engaged in much the same activity as she was. For a moment, before Susan lost her balance, their eyes met, and he smiled.

Warmth flooded through her. She grasped Gerrit's arm for support on one side and Deborah's on the other. "He's here." Her voice squeaked, and she swallowed. "Daire is here."

"Where?" Deborah rose to her toes. "I don't see—ah. He's approaching the happy couple."

Susan didn't waste more time trying to stand on her toes. She pushed through the crowd, apologizing when she jostled others but not stopping until she, too, reached the bride, groom, and Bridget McCorkle.

Daniel looked like his mother, with heavy dark hair and eyes too brilliant to be a true black. Their smiles matched, too.

The smiles of all three persons died the instant Susan propelled her way into the group around the newlyweds.

"Miss Morris," Bridget grumbled. "Could you not stay away another day?"

"No, I—"

Daire strode into the circle. Bridget grasped her son's arm and tried to draw him away. The young man stood his ground, his gaze fixed on Daire.

Susan watched Daire, too, wondering what he would do or say, every muscle in her body tense.

"Mr. McCorkle." Daire held out his hand to the young man. "I see I am to offer you felicitations."

"Ye–es, sir." Daniel McCorkle hesitated a moment then shook Daire's proffered hand. "Though I'm not sure—"

"Daire Grassick." Daire's smile set Susan's heart racing.

"And this is your lovely bride?" He bowed to the fair young lady beside Daniel. "May the Lord bless your union."

"Thank you, sir." She bowed her head. "We are honored to have you here. My father—" Her gaze darted around the courtyard.

"He's gone for more lemons," Daniel assured her. "He'll be back." He turned his attention to Daire and Susan right behind him. "We have more guests than we expected."

"I'm sure they wish to give you a good send-off to—" Daire cocked his head, as though he listened to something far away. "Iowa, is it, that Heath has land?"

"I—I dunno, sir." Daniel shifted from one foot to the other. "I'm not going to farm."

"He's going aboard my father's ship." The bride raised her head and her whole face lit. "When Daniel promised to do that, Father gave us his blessing to marry, but we had to do so right away." Her porcelain fair features turned begonia pink. "Because they ship out in three days, that is."

"You do?" Daire's shoulders jerked as though someone had struck him between the shoulder blades.

Susan felt the same impact in her middle. She caught her breath and took a step forward. "What have you done with the goldfinch, then?" she demanded before she could stop herself. "We thought you were going to sell it to Mr. Heath in exchange for land out west."

"I couldn't." Daniel gazed down at his bride. "She. . .um. . . fell in love with it, and when her father said there was work aboard the ship he is with, I—I let her keep it as a wedding present."

"And now you'll be wanting it back, won't you, Mr. Grassick?" Bridget's words emerged more challenge than query.

"Oh no," the younger Mrs. McCorkle cried. "You cannot. Daniel said you sold it."

Daire remained silent for several moments. Though the fiddles crooned and many danced, others watched the group around the bride and groom. Susan's stomach clenched so hard she feared she'd be sick. She understood if Daire wanted the goldfinch back, but the bride looked so stricken, the notion of taking away her gift seemed cruel. Yet it had been stolen.

"Mr. McCorkle," Daire spoke at last, "did you truly give up the prospect of land of your own so that your wife could have the goldfinch bottle?"

"Aye sir." Daniel held his head at a proud angle. "When I learned how my mother got it, and how you needed it, I'd have given it back, but you were gone, and when Pearl wanted it so bad, I couldn't bring myself to give it even to Miss Susan. But we'll give it up to you now that you have come for it. It's only right."

"Though it's ever so pretty." Pearl looked about to cry.

Daire glanced around the encircling crowd. His lips tilted in a half smile when he met Susan's gaze upon him; then he settled his glance on Pearl. "Mrs. McCorkle, you may keep the goldfinch. It was created to be given to a loved one, and that's what's been done with it. But please allow me to extricate what is inside it."

"There's something inside it?" Pearl asked.

"A slip of paper precious only to a few," Daire answered.

"Like Heath." Daniel looked dismayed, as though regretting not seeking for something inside, then smiled. "You won't damage the bottle?"

"I wouldn't think for a moment of doing so." Daire nodded.

"So it's mine?" Pearl breathed. "Then you can have whatever's in it whenever you like."

"Right away," Daniel added.

"It can wait," Bridget declared.

Daire nodded. "Yes, it can wait until after the celebrations. I have other, more important matters to tend to now."

Nearly sagging with relief and joy, Susan stepped away from the circle around the bride and groom. They hugged

Daire, along with Bridget, as though he were a member of the family. Since his arrival in the group, no one had noticed her. Once, this would have hurt her deeply, sent her scrambling for a way to get noticed. Now she simply smiled at the happy conclusion to Daire's situation and started back toward Deborah and Gerrit, with more courtesy this time.

"Thank You, Lord, for finding the goldfinch," she murmured beneath the noise of the crowd. "May Daire now find his purpose in—oh." A hand touched her arm, and she jumped, spun on her heel, and came face-to-face with Daire Grassick.

"I didn't mean to startle you." He gave her a tentative smile. "But you were running away."

"I wasn't running." Susan's voice sounded breathless to her ears. "I—you—I was thanking the Lord for making everything work out for you."

"He has indeed worked matters out for my family."

"Except you lost the goldfinch."

"I didn't lose it. I gave it away to someone who wanted it more than a secure future because her beloved gave it to her."

"I know, but—" Susan's throat closed, and her eyes burned. "Your family," she managed in a whisper.

"We'd already given it up as lost for good."

"You could have taken it back."

"No, I couldn't. My grandfather said the goldfinch had caused strife in the family, when it was to symbolize love and constancy, and we needed to be rid of it, give it up to the Lord." He tucked her hand into the crook of his elbow and turned toward the side of the courtyard. "Will you walk with me?"

"Deborah and Gerrit are here, too."

"I see them. They won't miss us for a bit." He turned his head to the left.

Deborah and Gerrit had joined those dancing to the lively music.

Susan laughed. "They look so happy. I expect theirs will be the next wedding I attend."

"Perhaps." Daire covered her hand with his free one and guided her through the throng to where a narrow street led out of the courtyard. "Perhaps not theirs, if I can change your mind."

"If you—" Susan stopped and faced him in the darkness. "What are you saying?"

"Too much, or perhaps just in the wrong order." He rested his hands on her shoulders. "Let me start with this: Susan Morris, I am not a man of many talents. I failed at farming and glassmaking and never trained for a profession, unlike the rest of my family. But I could have stayed there forever, even taken a wife there, and never wanted for anything."

"But you haven't?" Susan could hardly speak her chest felt so constricted.

"I was hiding there, hiding from my own fear of making more mistakes instead of trusting in the Lord to guide me. Your telegram guided me right back here." He moved his warm hands to cup the sides of her face. "I've known what I wanted for days now, but I was afraid." He laughed. "I'm still afraid."

"Of what?" she whispered.

"You're an heiress, Susan, and although I get a share of the profits from the family business quarterly, it's not anything like your inheritance, and that's why I left."

"You left because I'm an heiress?" Indignation loosened Susan's tongue. "If that isn't the most absurd thing I've ever heard. That money is to help me catch a husband, not lose me one. I mean—that is. . . Oh, dear. I've spoken out of turn."

"Not at all," Daire said.

Then he kissed her. Though the music behind them rose in a jig, on fiddles, Susan thought it sounded more like a concerto with a full orchestra. She crushed Daire's neck cloth between her hands and would have sagged at the knees if Daire hadn't held her upright.

"I love you," he murmured with his lips a fraction of an inch from hers. "Will you be my wife?"

"Maybe."

"Maybe?" He jerked back. "You just let me kiss you."

"I suppose that was bad of me." Susan ducked her head, and her hair tumbled loose around her face and shoulders. "I've so been hoping you would, I forgot. You see, Daire—" She peered at him through the curtain of her hair. "I want to work with the people here, help young men like that baby's father and Daniel McCorkle and the young women, too, to find work and settle where they can have better lives. Do the things Heath promises to do but never does. I have the money, but only if I get married to a man who agrees to use it for this purpose." She tilted her head flirtatiously. "And I don't know where to find such a man."

"Minx." Daire laughed and kissed the tip of her nose. "You can stop searching if you're willing."

"I'm willing." She rested her head on his shoulder. "If you're asking me to marry you, then the answer is I will."

A Letter To Our Readers

Dear Reader:

In order that we might better contribute to your reading enjoyment, we would appreciate your taking a few minutes to respond to the following questions. We welcome your comments and read each form and letter we receive. When completed, please return to the following:

Fiction Editor
Heartsong Presents
PO Box 719
Uhrichsville, Ohio 44683

1. Did you enjoy reading *The Heiress* by Laurie Alice Eakes?
   ❏ Very much! I would like to see more books by this author!
   ❏ Moderately. I would have enjoyed it more if

   _____

   _____

   _____

2. Are you a member of **Heartsong Presents**? ❏ Yes ❏ No
   If no, where did you purchase this book? _____

   _____

3. How would you rate, on a scale from 1 (poor) to 5 (superior), the cover design? _____

4. On a scale from 1 (poor) to 10 (superior), please rate the following elements.

   ____ Heroine   ____ Plot
   ____ Hero   ____ Inspirational theme
   ____ Setting   ____ Secondary characters

5. These characters were special because? _____

_____

_____

6. How has this book inspired your life? _____

_____

_____

7. What settings would you like to see covered in future
   Heartsong Presents books? _____

_____

_____

8. What are some inspirational themes you would like to see
   treated in future books? _____

_____

_____

9. Would you be interested in reading other **Heartsong
   Presents** titles? ❑ Yes   ❑ No

10. Please check your age range:
   ❑ Under 18   ❑ 18-24
   ❑ 25-34   ❑ 35-45
   ❑ 46-55   ❑ Over 55

Name _____

Occupation _____

Address _____

City, State, Zip _____

E-mail _____

WILDFLOWER HEARTS

3 stories in 1

Three siblings each face interesting predicaments in the untamed Badlands.

Historical, paperback, 352 pages, 5⁵⁄₁₆" x 8"

Hearts♥ng

Presents

Great Inspirational Romance at a Great Price!

Heartsong Presents books are inspirational romances in contemporary and historical settings, designed to give you an enjoyable, spirit-lifting reading experience. You can choose wonderfully written titles from some of today's best authors like Wanda E. Brunstetter, Mary Connealy, Susan Page Davis, Cathy Marie Hake, Joyce Livingston, and many others.

When ordering quantities less than twelve, above titles are $2.97 each.
Not all titles may be available at time of order.